's

1

'The big man grabbed Dick and by brute force removed his grasp on Flick's wrist. Uncle Bob was still on the ground. Tony was struggling with the third man, Harris. Flick leaped to his feet and there was a gleam of light as the knife flashed round in his hand.'

One bright Saturday morning Kevin, his sister Sandra, and their friend Dick, are wandering about the gloomy northern streets they call the Jungle, hoping for something interesting to happen – and it does, with a vengeance. First their aunt and uncle disappear, and then, before the week is over, they've done a moonlight flit, made a secret home for themselves and their young cousins in a deserted warehouse, stumbled on to the secret of a highly organized criminal gang, are besieged and then kidnapped by the villains, and finally manage to solve the mystery and capture the criminals *almost* unaided.

This is a fast-moving, exciting story about interesting people in dilemmas many of which might really have happened.

Also in Puffins: *Good-bye to Gumble's Yard, Noah's Castle, Top of the World, Hell's Edge* and *The Intruder.*

John Rowe Townsend

Gumble's Yard

Illustrated by Dick Hart

Puffin Books
by arrangement with Hutchinson of London

Puffin Books, Penguin Books Ltd, Harmondsworth, Middlesex, England
Penguin Books, 625 Madison Avenue, New York, New York 10022, U.S.A
Penguin Books Australia Ltd, Ringwood, Victoria, Australia
Penguin Books Canada Ltd, 2801 John Street, Markham, Ontario, Canada l 3R 1B4
Penguin Books (N.Z.) Ltd, 182 190 Wairau Road, Auckland 10, New Zealand

First published by Hutchinson 1961
Published in Puffin Books 1967
Reprinted 1970 (twice), 1971, 1973, 1974, 1975, 1976, 1977, 1979,
1980 (twice), 1982, 1983

Made and printed in Great Britain by
Hazell Watson & Viney Ltd, Aylesbury, Bucks
Set in Linotype Georgian

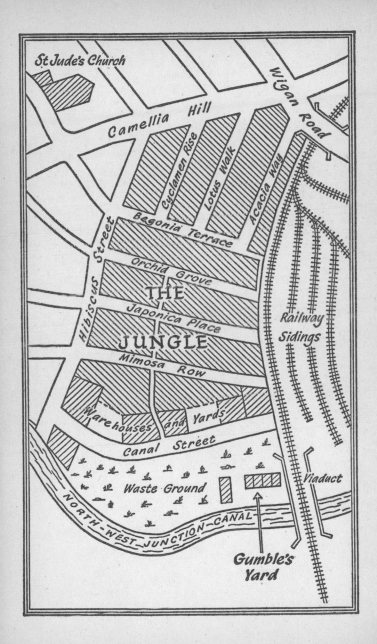

1 IT was a fine spring day, not warm but with a sort of hazy sunshine, and I was walking through the Jungle with my sister Sandra and my friend Dick. The Jungle isn't a real jungle, it's a district off the Wigan Road in the city of Cobchester. We call it the Jungle because all the streets are named after tropical flowers – like Orchid Grove, where we live. That may sound gay and colourful, but there's nothing colourful about the Jungle. It's a dirty old place, and one of these days the Corporation are going to pull it all down – if it doesn't fall down of its own accord first.

But on this sunny Saturday morning, as we walked home to dinner, even the Jungle seemed a cheerful place. Summer was coming, the blades of grass were showing between the stone setts, and soon the weeds would blossom on the empty sites. The days were getting longer. Next week perhaps we would be playing cricket after school. There was a dog in Mimosa Row that I was getting very friendly with. I was going to make a soap-box car for my cousin Harold. Life was full of interesting things to do.

We walked three abreast, with Sandra in the middle. And as we turned into Orchid Grove I felt happy and burst out singing.

'Hark at him!' said Sandra. 'Not a care in the world.'

'Poor old Kevin!' said Dick, with mock sympathy. 'He's got a pain. Where does it hurt, Kevin?'

'I'll hurt *you* in a minute!' I said.

'Oh yes? You and who else?'

'Do you think I couldn't?'

'Yes, I do think you couldn't.'

'Well, I'll show you.' And we started a friendly scuffle, the kind that happens a dozen times a day.

I generally get the worse of any fight with Dick. He's fourteen, a year older than I am, and quite a bit bigger. He's a cheerful red-headed boy, very good-looking, and the only thing wrong with him is that he's bossy. He thinks he's a born leader (which he may be) and he thinks he's always right (which he isn't). And now he held me off with one hand, grinning in a way that he knew would annoy me.

'Break it up, you two!' said Sandra. Small and thin, with sharp determined face, she stepped between us. 'Fight when you're on your own, not when you're with me. Kevin, what did you start it for? It was all your fault.'

Sandra always blames me – partly because I'm her brother and partly because in her eyes Dick can do no wrong.

8

'Just wait a minute, Sandra,' said Dick. 'Give me time to bash his brains out. Oh no, I was forgetting, he hasn't any. ...'

'Oh, leave off!' said Sandra again; and then, as something caught her eye, she added, 'Just look what's happening over there!'

Dick and I broke it up, and looked the way she was pointing.

Along the other side of the street came the two grown-ups from our house. First, Doris, in her best coat and headscarf, stalking ahead as fast as she could walk. Then Walter, with a battered suitcase, scurrying after her.

Walter is our uncle. When our parents died Sandra and I went to live with Walter and his two young children, Harold and Jean. Walter's wife had left him, and Sandra had to act as mother to the younger ones. It was hard work for her. She's only twelve herself.

When Doris, a friend of Walter's, came to live with us, it looked as though things might get better. But not for long. Doris was a blonde, bulky woman with a round, puddingy face. She was always padding about the house in slippers, a cigarette in her mouth, grousing and not getting anything done. She didn't like us children, and she tried to take it out on Walter. Every few days they'd have a row and she'd threaten to go away.

'I'm leaving you,' she'd say. 'I'm not staying in this house another minute.'

'All right, then,' Walter would say. 'Hop it, and good riddance.'

He knew she wouldn't hop it, because she'd nowhere else to go.

'You'll say that once too often, Walter Thompson,' she'd tell him, and then she'd go on grumbling: 'What with you and them brats, it's enough to drive me barmy. ...' But it would all die down. By evening they'd be round at the George, the pub in the next street, just as if nothing had happened. Sandra would put Harold and Jean to bed, and then she and I would sit up and do what we liked for a bit, until Walter and Doris came back.

But now, this Saturday midday, the two of them were hurrying along Orchid Grove in a very strange manner. Doris strode ahead, looking neither left nor right. Walter caught up with her and tried to say something, but she ignored him. Neither of them took any notice of us.

I was mildly puzzled. 'What's up with them?' I said. 'I've never seen them go off like this before. And at dinner-time, too.'

Sandra looked quite alarmed. She ran across the street and caught Doris by the arm.

'Will you be out for dinner?' she asked.

Doris shook herself free. 'I will that!' she said fiercely.

'What shall we have?'

'You can fend for yourself, can't you?'

'When will you be back?' asked Sandra.

But Walter had now caught up. 'Ask no questions and you'll be told no lies!' he snapped. 'Now get o' t'road!'

And the two of them – Doris with her head in the air, and Walter hurrying alongside, still trying to make her listen to him – turned out of Orchid Grove into Hibiscus Street.

As they disappeared round the corner, three

or four heads poked out of doorways, and puzzled or knowing looks were exchanged. I shrugged my shoulders.

'They might keep their quarrels to themselves, instead of putting on a show for the neighbours,' I said.

But Sandra still looked anxious.

'There's something behind all this,' she said. 'I've felt for a few days there was real trouble coming. And this has got me worried.'

'Cheer up, love,' said Dick. 'Look on the bright side. They're out of the way for a bit. Enjoy the peace while you've got it.'

'I wish I felt sure it was only a bit,' said Sandra.

'Well, they wouldn't walk out on you, would they?'

'I don't know,' said Sandra thoughtfully, 'I don't know. .... Anyway, come on, Kevin, we'd better get something to eat.'

'And I'd better get home,' said Dick. He lives just the other side of Hibiscus Street. 'Don't worry, they'll turn up like a pair of bad pennies. See you later.' And off he went whistling.

We went into the house. The younger children, Harold and Jean, had appeared from nowhere and were squabbling mildly in the kitchen.

'Give us a butty, Sandra!' urged Jean. She danced around us, twirling her skirt, a roly-poly, round-faced, cheeky child of six.

'A butty, a butty, a red jam butty!' she chanted. I aimed a clout at her, but missed.

Harold slouched off into a chair and said nothing. At eight he was almost the image of his father Walter: small, slightly built, with wispy fair hair and blue eyes. He seemed to have gone 12 off into his private dream world; but after a minute he got up again and went to the cupboard. He took out a big loaf and put it on the table between Sandra and Jean as if to quieten the row once and for all.

Sandra took the breadknife, and in a minute had sent the two children out with a thick slice of bread and jam in each hand. Then, putting the kettle on, she turned to me.

'I bet they've hooked it!' she said savagely. 'I bet they've hooked it!'

'I don't think Walter would walk out on us,' I said. 'In fact I don't really think Doris would. You know what she is. All talk. She's always planning to do this and that, but nothing ever comes of it. I don't know what they're up to, but I bet they'll be at the George tonight as usual.'

But I didn't feel quite as confident as I tried to sound. I remembered that Doris had been particularly cross and shrill for the last few days. It had begun when Walter came home one evening and said he'd been offered a job in Yorkshire but he'd turned it down because there wouldn't be anywhere for us to live. Doris was furious and had been taking it out of everybody ever since. She'd kept saying she was sick of this house and sick of this town and sick of him and sick of us. What if she'd really gone? And if so, had Walter gone too?

I comforted myself with what Dick had said. Surely they'd be coming back. It was common sense after all. And by the time I'd eaten a few slices of bread and jam and drunk a mug of tea I felt much better.

13   Afterwards I went to the football match with

Dick and his father, while Sandra saw to some mending and the youngsters played out in the street. It was a splendid match, the last day of the league championship, and United won 3–1. They were top of the table already, and this last performance capped it all. I came home full of the afternoon's play and hoarse with shouting, and I'd quite forgotten we had any worries.

Saturday tea time was usually the high point of the week at 40 Orchid Grove. Walter generally went to the match too – though he never took me with him – and Doris went to see a friend, and they both used to come home for a hot tea before going round to the George to spend the evening. It would be a good tea with sausages or beans or tomatoes, and there'd be a big fire, and if United had won Walter would be in a happy mood. He'd even been known to hand out sixpences and shillings (which we spent at once in case he tried to take them back next day).

But today was a chilly contrast. There was no fire in the hearth, no meal on the table. As I stood in the doorway, my spirits sinking, Sandra came in from the street with a child on each hand. She looked grim but calm.

'Light a fire, Kevin, if there's some coal,' she said. 'We're on our own this evening.'

Everybody was hungry. After having only a bread-and-jam dinner, Harold and Jean were whimpering a bit and wiping their faces with grubby hands. So we had a good look round to see what there was to eat, and we found quite a lot of things. There was some bacon that was probably a bit off, but not bad. There were potatoes. There was a whole jar of jam. There were several milk bottles with varying amounts of milk in the bottom, all gone sour. But there was a tin of condensed milk and there was plenty of tea. In fact the cupboard was better stocked than usual. And we had one surprising bit of luck. We found a ten-shilling note under the tea-jar that Doris must have forgotten. Sandra pocketed that. 'You never know when we'll need it,' she said.

We had coal and candles too, so really we were much better off than we might have been. There was no electricity in the house, and we'd no shillings for the gas, but I soon made a good fire and we had a fine fry up of bacon and potatoes. There was enough for us all to feel full. Then we stoked the fire up again and sat round it.

'Tell us a story, Kevin,' said Sandra. So I made up a story, all about children cast away on a desert island. And we imagined it was us, and that we could hear the waves beating all round us. And we pretended to be alone and in peril, instead of warm and comfortable in our home at Cobchester. I went on with the story for quite a while, because once I get started it's no trouble to make up stories. They just come to me. But after a while we noticed that Jean was nodding, and Harold was getting tired too. So Sandra told them both to go to bed. Then there was a lot of arguing, and Jean cheeked both of us, and Sandra belted her, not hard, but she squawked as if she was being murdered. And Harold did a go-slow and took twenty minutes to get his shoes and socks off, and every time we looked the other way he stopped getting undressed and did something else. And even when they were in bed in a corner of the room they kept grousing and cheeking us and pinching each other and bawling, and it was a long time before we got any peace.

In the end they both went to sleep. We didn't know the time, but it was getting dark. By now I had persuaded myself that Walter and Doris would be in the pub as usual, and I told Sandra so.

'Well, if they are, they won't come out before closing-time,' said Sandra.

'Dick was right, it's peaceful without them,' I said. I'd quite enjoyed my evening. 'It won't be peaceful when they come in, though.'

We both grimaced, for this was the one drawback to Saturday. Not that Walter and Doris were violent when they came home on Saturday night, like a couple we knew in the next street, but there was often a lot of shouting and quarrelling, and Sandra and I would get cuffed if we put a foot wrong, or even sometimes if we didn't.

So we decided we would go to bed, to be out of the way.

Our house, like all the others in Orchid Grove, had a living-room and a scullery and two bedrooms. Our back bedroom was in a bad state because the roof needed repairing, so we four children all slept downstairs in the living-room. We had a big iron bedstead, and Harold and I slept with our heads at one end and Sandra and Jean at the other. There was room for all of us, and we had some blankets and old coats to keep us warm, and it was a very good arrangement. Sandra and I were awake for quite a time, listening to footsteps going past and people singing and shouting, and wondering whether Walter and Doris were coming. Then Sandra fell asleep, but I lay quietly watching the red embers in the grate and thinking how well we'd managed. And eventually I dozed off too, and I didn't know anything more until next morning.

Sandra was shaking me. 'They haven't come!' she said. 'They haven't come!'

2 THE younger children were awake and were racketing round the house. They didn't seem to have noticed anything amiss. Sandra and I looked at each other in dismay.

'What if they've been in an accident?' said Sandra. 'Or got into trouble?'

'I don't think so,' I said. 'We should have had the police round. I expect they've had a heavy night. They'll be sleeping it off somewhere. They're sure to be home some time today.'

But even as I said it I felt they wouldn't. I remembered once again the things Doris had said. I knew how unreliable Walter was. I had a picture in my mind that was all too convincing, of Walter and Doris hitching a lift into Yorkshire and planning to make a fresh start without us.

'If they're not back tonight,' I said, 'we'll have to go to the police, or the Cruelty.'

'Mmm,' said Sandra. She didn't sound at all

certain. We were both thinking hard as we got tea and bread-and-jam ready for breakfast.

'If we did that, what would happen?' asked Sandra after a while.

I didn't know what would happen. I supposed we would be 'taken into care', as the phrase went, but I'd only the cloudiest idea of what this meant. I imagined us being questioned by police and officials and welfare workers. I pictured us in some chilly institution or being farmed out upon foster-parents we didn't like. Worst of all, I imagined us being split up and sent to different places.

'Oh, let's look after ourselves,' I said, 'for the time being, anyway. Walter and Doris may still come back. If they're not here in a few days' time we can think again.'

I realize now that this decision was wrong. We ought to have sought help that very day. But it didn't seem right at the time. To tell the truth, we were really rather afraid of police and officials, because all we had ever had to do with them was being told off for some mischief or other. Then, we were used to fending for ourselves a good deal already, and it did not seem as difficult as it might have done to children who were used to being looked after more than we were. And, finally, the thought had already crossed my mind that if the worst came to the worst I would try to find my Uncle Bob. But I will come back to that later.

Anyway, Sandra and I decided we would try to keep the home together. It was surprising at first how little the younger ones were worried. At breakfast Harold hardly spoke. He was in his private dream-world again – halfway to the moon this time. Harold had invented a special kind of moon rocket that worked by magnetic repulsion. This got it off the earth, and also prevented it from crashing on to the moon when it arrived there. Harold spent most of his days shooting back and forth in space, with suitable noises and gestures. In his day-dreams he was Sir Harold Thompson, the great scientist-explorer, continually reporting new discoveries to the Queen (he hadn't time to bother with underlings like the Prime Minister). In real life it was another matter, and he would be glad enough of the push-cart I was going to make him.

Jean, on the other hand, had a certain amount to say.

'Where's Auntie Doris?' she demanded, as she walked round the room with her bread in one hand and her mug of tea in the other.

'Gone visiting,' said Sandra. 'Sit down.'

'Who's she visiting? I never heard of anybody going visiting at Sunday breakfast-time. Has she gone for good? I bet she's gone for good.'

'We don't know,' said Sandra. 'I expect she'll be back.'

'I bet she won't,' said Jean, taking a huge bite of bread-and-jam. 'And I don't care if she doesn't. My dad can come back, but I don't want her.'

'Jean!' said Sandra, shocked. 'Don't say such naughty things!'

'Don't care, don't care, don't care!' sang Jean, with her mouth full. I aimed another clout at her, and this time I connected, but it didn't have any effect. 'Don't care, so there! So there, don't care,' she chanted, dancing out of range.

'It's all right for *her*!' said Sandra grimly.

'Will you be our auntie now?' asked Jean with interest. 'You'd be good at it, I bet. I'd rather have you than her.'

'Shut up!' said Sandra. 'I told you, we don't know that she's gone. And, listen, don't tell anyone we're on our own, or I'll scrag you.'

After breakfast Jean and Harold went out: Jean to play with a pal of hers from up the street and Harold on a trip to the planet Neptune, for which the point of departure was a launching-pad he'd built with planks in a warehouse yard in Hibiscus Street. Sandra and I stayed in the house for a while talking about our problem but not really getting anywhere.

'Let's go and see Dick,' Sandra suggested after a while.

This seemed the best idea. We always went to Dick with our problems anyway. He'd always know what to do, and he'd be ready to take charge. In face there'd be no stopping him. At one time when there was a feud between boys from our district and those of St Jude's, at the other side of Camellia Hill, Dick took charge of the Jungle Army. We generally won, too, but the feud had now almost petered out because a new curate came to St Jude's Church and got everybody there busy with organized games and youth clubs and dramatics.

We knocked at the door of Dick's house. His mother came, and didn't look any too pleased. We heard her shouting something to her husband about 'them Thompson children'. We were 22 never very popular with respectable people in the district, because ours was a very poor home, and Walter and Doris were not much liked. But Dick's father was kind and asked us in, and patted Sandra on the cheek and said, 'How do, love?' And he asked us if we had had any breakfast, at which Dick's mother pursed her lips a little.

'Y'd have me feeding all t'lame ducks in t'neighbourhood, you would,' she said to her husband. But then she turned to us and said, 'Well, have you?' and we knew she would have given us something.

I said firmly that we'd had our breakfast. Mrs Hedley began muttering something uncomplimentary about Walter and Doris, but we didn't catch what it was. Just then Dick appeared, so we all got out of the house rather quickly, and Dick came round to Orchid Grove with us. We told him what had happened. Dick whistled.

'Left you high and dry after all, eh?' he said. 'I thought they would.' (This wasn't what he'd thought at all, but we didn't remind him.) And his first reaction was pretty well what I'd expected. 'You'd better go to the police. Or, if you like, I'll ask my dad to go.'

So we explained why we didn't want that. There was a good deal of argument, from which it was clear that Dick had no more idea than we had of what would happen if we reported our difficulties. In the end he seemed to come round to our point of view.

'But you've got a lot of problems, haven't you?' he said. 'Food, money, school, the neighbours. . . . To begin with, what are you going to live on?'

We told him we still had some tea and bread-and-jam, but only enough for the midday meal.

'But we've got ten shillings,' Sandra said. 'We can go to the Jewish shop, that's open on Sundays, and get something for tea.'

'You want to save your money,' said Dick. 'I'll tell you what we'll do. You two can come to tea with me, and we'll put food in our pockets for the others while nobody's looking.'

Sandra and I were both doubtful, but Dick went straight on.

'Ten shillings won't go far, anyway,' he said. 'You need an income. You'll have to get a job, Kevin. And the only kind of job you can get is a paper round.'

'That's not so easily got,' I said. 'Not in this district, anyway.'

'You can have my job at Mould's,' said Dick. 'I'll take you there in the morning. I'll say I'm giving up and you can have my round.'

This was generous of Dick, because we knew he was saving up for a bicycle. But he didn't stop to be thanked.

'You'll need more than that,' he went on. 'I'll think of something soon. Now, what about the rent tomorrow?'

'The rent's up to date,' said Sandra, 'and they'll let it run for a week or two.'

'You can't stay long, anyway,' Dick pointed out. 'Somebody will soon notice that you're on your own.'

Now this of course was quite true. Not that ours was one of the houses where people are dropping in all the time. Our neighbours gener-ally felt that the less they saw of Walter and 24

Doris the better they liked them. But Orchid Grove is a great place for curiosity. And just at that moment, as if it had been arranged to prove the point, there was a rat-tat at the door and old Mrs Grimshaw from across the street put her head in.

'All on yer own, eh?' she said. 'All on yer own?'

'Yes,' I said coldly.

There was a moment's pause. Then:

'Where are they?'

Now there was a time when I might have been cheeky and said, 'Mind you own business.' But I had been thinking hard as she spoke, and I had decided I would have to tell a lie in the most matter-of-fact way I could.

'Gone to my Uncle Bob's in Ledford,' I said.

'Gone to Ledford, eh? Left you on your own, eh? All four of you, eh? Little uns an' all?' She spoke in a disapproving tone, but not an unbelieving one. 'And when will they be back?'

I was just going to say I didn't exactly know when Sandra chipped in and said in a very confident voice, 'They'll be back tonight.'

'Oh,' said Mrs Grimshaw. 'Just a nice little week-end jaunt. Well, there's some that can take their responsibilities lightly, I must say.' She looked more disapproving than ever. But she spoke quite kindly. 'Well, if y' want aught you can just come across t'street,' she said, and withdrew.

'Why did you say that?' I asked crossly.

'She'd have been round to the Cruelty right away,' said Sandra. 'I could see it in her eye. I wouldn't be surprised if she went even now.'

25

We looked out of the window and saw Mrs Grimshaw disappearing into her own house.

'Well, she's not gone straight there,' I said. 'But it'll be all round the district pretty soon.'

'The fact is,' said Dick, 'that you'll have to move tonight.'

'Tonight!' I echoed, but Sandra, who was sharper on the uptake, was merely nodding. 'Tonight!' I repeated. 'But where can we go?'

'I was just thinking about that,' said Dick. 'There's only one place for you. Gumble's Yard.'

'Gumble's Yard!' we both gasped. I was sure that Sandra went white. 'Gumble's Yard!'

3 GUMBLE'S YARD had been empty for at least
a year. It was right down at the bottom end of
the Jungle, in the bend of the old North-West
Junction Canal. You got to it by way of Canal
Street, and it was the farthest point from the
main road – a complete dead end. It was just a
row of four cottages, with one or two outbuild-
ings, which at one time belonged to a warehouse.
In the days when the canal was in use the whole
place was called Gumble's Wharf. During the
war some bombs fell near by; and the warehouse
was badly shaken and had to be pulled down,
but the cottages were left because there were
people living in them. But now all the people
had gone.

We were dismayed when Dick suggested that
we should move down there.

'Oh, Dick!' said Sandra. 'We couldn't. Not
with the young ones. Why, it's in an awful state –
27 nearly falling down, I should think. And there

wouldn't be any light or water. Besides, it's a long way from the nearest houses that are lived in. We wouldn't feel safe.'

'Wait a minute, wait a minute,' said Dick. 'I know it's a long way from the nearest houses, but that's all to the good, because you're less likely to be seen. Nobody goes down there, and there's no reason why anybody should. As for the other objections, well, there's something I'd like to show you. A secret. Let's go there now.'

So we did. We walked down the length of Hibiscus Street and turned into Canal Street, which is just about the deadest street I know, because since the canal went out of use there isn't really any reason for it to exist. At the side away from the canal there are still a few old buildings – warehouses and stabling and so on – but all disused and crumbling away. At the other side, there is just open space between the street and the canal. To get to Gumble's Yard you go right along Canal Street, almost to where it's cut off by the railway viaduct, and then you cross an open site about two hundred yards wide.

It took us about ten minutes to get there. And although it was another fine morning the place certainly looked pretty dismal.

The actual structure still seemed fairly solid, but the four cottages had not a door between them, and all the downstairs windows were broken. Inside was a good deal of rubbish but not much else. It seemed as if everything that could possibly be looted had been taken away. There was a nasty dank smell. We looked round for a minute or two, and then Sandra turned to Dick and I could see that she was just going to 28 tell him the whole idea was impossible. But Dick was all smiles.

'Don't say it!' he told her. 'I'm going to show you my secret. This will surprise you.'

He led us outside, and round to the far end of the row of cottages. Here the gable end faced on to the supports of the railway viaduct. It was a dark, isolated corner, and not overlooked – not even from the railway, as the angle was too sharp.

'Look up,' said Dick. So we looked up at the end wall of the cottages, and high in the gable end we saw a door, an ordinary closed door, but very odd-looking because there was nothing in front of it except a twenty-foot drop to the ground. Beside it was a grime-encrusted window.

'That door,' said Dick, 'belongs to an attic that runs over the tops of all four cottages. At one time it must have had something to do with the wharf, but the earliest thing I can remember was that old man Kite lived there. He was a bit queer in the head, and never spoke to anybody. In his day you got to that door by a sort of iron staircase, like a fire escape, but after he died they pulled that down.'

'Can you get in now?' I asked.

'Watch,' said Dick. He shinned up the drainpipe at the corner of the block. Then, sidestepping where a missing brick gave him a toehold, he reached with one hand for a bracket which must formerly have held a lamp. Transferring the other hand to the bracket, he was able to reach the window-frame. To our surprise the window moved easily, and in a moment Dick was wriggling through. Seconds later the door opened and Dick stood in the doorway looking down at us.

'How's that?' he asked.

'Terrific,' said Sandra sardonically. 'You ought to get a job in a circus. But do you expect us all to do that?'

'Certainly not,' said Dick. He disappeared from view, and the next thing to emerge was the end of a decorator's ladder, which Dick proceeded to lower to the ground.

Sandra stared. I burst into laughter.

'How on earth did you get that?' I demanded.

'Come up here and I'll tell you,' said Dick. So we went up, and Dick drew the ladder up behind us and closed the door.

The attic was long and narrow, and you could only stand upright in the middle of it. It had three windows, but they were all thick with dirt and it was pretty dark inside. It smelt much drier than down below, though, and the floor seemed sound. Inside were a camp bed, two or three old chairs, some packing-cases, and a couple of rugs. There was also a paraffin stove. Our astonishment grew.

'Bill Berry and I found this place,' Dick said. 'Bill's in the Army now, but I used to go around with him quite a bit before he joined up. We weren't going to tell anyone about it, but I know Bill wouldn't mind, seeing you're in such a fix.'

'Did you bring all these things in?'

'Not all of them,' said Dick. 'It was a bit strange. The camp bed and a chair and one or two cases were here when we first came, and the ladder too. Somebody must have used the place before us. But it must have been quite a while 30 ago, because everything was covered with dust. And we've not seen any signs of anybody coming here since. So I shouldn't worry about that.'

'Was there anything to show who it might have been?'

'There was practically nothing,' said Dick. 'Cigarette packets, a page of a letter addressed to somebody called – now, what was it? – Flick. And a piece cut from a newspaper of nearly a year ago, something about a Lady Westley. Well, I don't know who Flick is, but he doesn't come here now. If you could have seen that dust ... Bill and I brought a broom and a scrubbing-brush and bucket – they're still here, in that corner – and we got it really cleaned up. We brought the other chairs and the stove, too. We were going to make it a private den, but there isn't really anything much to do down here, you know – it's so quiet, and nobody goes past.'

'When were you last here?'

'Oh, two or three weeks ago, when Bill was on leave.'

Sandra had been looking round thoughtfully while I asked the questions. 'It's not a bad place,' she admitted. 'But what about water? And how are we all going to get in and out? Maybe Kevin can climb up the way you did, but I can't and I'm sure the younger ones can't. And the ladder isn't much good if it's up above and we're down below.'

But Dick had an answer for everything. Although at the start he had seemed doubtful about our idea of fending for ourselves, he was now getting enthusiastic.

'You can get water from a standpipe in one of

the outhouses,' he said. 'I'll show you later how to do it. There's a lot of lumber in there, too, and I think I know how we can make use of that. As for getting in and out, well, look at this.'

He led us to a corner of the room and, with a conjurer's gesture, lifted one of the rugs. We saw that it covered a trapdoor. 'Here's your future route,' he said. 'Bill and I found this when we scrubbed the floor. You couldn't see it before for dust and grime. At the moment you can get down but not up, but we'll soon cure that.'

Dick lowered himself through the trapdoor, hung on with his hands for a moment, and dropped to the floor below. I followed, bending my knees as I landed. We were now in the bedroom of the end cottage. The trapdoor was in a dark corner of the cracked and dirty ceiling, and nobody would notice it when closed.

As Dick had said, you could get down but not up. But halfway up the adjoining wall was a heavy old-fashioned mantelpiece. 'You see,' said Dick, 'all we want is a really strong bracket, right up in the corner, to serve the same purpose as that lamp-bracket outside. Then you'll be able to stand on the mantelpiece, reach over to the bracket, and hang on to it while you push the trapdoor up. It won't be difficult because we'll get an old wooden box that can be the first step to the mantelpiece. Harold can do it quite easily. Jean might need a bit of help.'

'Where will we get the bracket?' I asked.

'I can pick up just the thing in Fred Appleby's yard,' said Dick. 'I'll have a word with him at dinner-time. And, come to think of it, it must be getting on for dinner-time now.'

We helped Sandra to come down through the trap. She was grousing a bit, and muttering something about having to be a family of Tarzans. But I could see that really she was quite impressed.

'You'll have a front door *and* a back,' said Dick cheerfully. 'Might be useful some time.' And he didn't know how right he was, for later on it was to be more useful than we could have guessed.

Sandra and I went back to Orchid Grove. We still half expected to find Walter and Doris there. But there was no sign of them. Harold had returned from his trip to Neptune and was lying on the bedstead reading a battered science-fiction magazine. Sandra hauled Jean in from the street, and we ate what dinner we could find. We finished up all the bits and pieces, including the stale ends of two or three loaves, and all that remained was some tea and half a jar of jam. But of course we still had the ten shillings.

After dinner, Sandra told the younger children what we were doing. She said it was only for a day or two, and then either Walter and Doris would come back or somebody else would look after us. To our surprise Harold took it rather badly. He suddenly came back to earth from all his space dreams, and blubbered a bit about wanting his dad. But Jean was not at all worried.

'I told you, I told you,' she cried. 'Sandra's the auntie now. We'll have a lovely time, Harold, you're a cry-baby. Poor little boy, wants his daddy....'

Harold lashed out at her through his tears. I
felt sorry for him. Unlike Jean, he was old

enough to feel the full weight of being abandoned, and unlike Sandra and myself he wasn't big enough to stand on his own feet. I didn't really feel too confident myself that we could manage. But a few minutes later Dick came in, full of confidence, and then I felt better. He had a bracket and a big hammer and some sand and cement as well. All five of us went down to Gumble's Yard.

There was still nobody about, either there or in Canal Street. The silence, in fact, seemed almost uncanny. Once again, Dick climbed into the attic from outside, but this time he reached down through the trapdoor and helped Sandra and the children up from the cottage bedroom. Then he came down through the trap himself, and he and I made a really good job of fixing the bracket.

Harold had whimpered a bit on the way down from Orchid Grove, but now the novelty of our proceedings took his mind off his troubles for a while. There was some discussion about what we should call our attic. Dick and Bill Berry had merely called it their den, but we didn't feel that was dignified enough. Jean wanted to call it Fairmead, a name she had seen over a house, but nobody else thought that was suitable either. Harold suggested the Spaceship – a part that no doubt the attic could play quite well in his imagination. But in the end we settled on Sandra's choice, which was the Homestead.

When the bracket was fixed, Harold and Jean wanted to practise getting up and down, but Dick insisted that it would have to be left to dry out. Sandra had decided that the attic was still 34 not clean enough, so she and Dick got busy scrubbing it.

'You'll have to do a moonlight flit tonight,' said Dick, 'and bring whatever you need from the other house down here. The sooner you get clear of Orchid Grove the safer you'll be. I'll sneak out at midnight and help you. What is there to bring?'

'Well, we'll have to bring the bedstead,' said Sandra, 'and the table, and we could do with another couple of chairs. Then there's that chest of drawers, and pots and pans and clothes and blankets. . . .'

'H'm. Quite an order,' said Dick. 'How are we going to carry all those things?'

'We've an old pram,' I said, 'that Jean used to sleep in until she got too big.'

'Just the job for the small stuff,' said Dick. 'I don't know about furniture, though. I'll talk to Fred Appleby again and see if I can borrow his hand-cart. Kevin, could you take Harold and Jean and bring some of the smaller things along now?'

'Fair enough,' I said. So the three of us went back to Orchid Grove and filled the old pram with clothes and blankets and anything else that could be packed in tightly and tidily. We didn't worry about anyone suspecting anything, because in the Jungle people are always pushing things about in old prams, and it's such a commonplace sight it's hardly noticed. Of course, if we were making several journeys with tables and chairs and pieces of bedstead it might be another matter. We couldn't do that in broad daylight.

35   We wheeled our load down Hibiscus Street

and turned into Canal Street. And there we had a surprise. Coming towards us from the direction of Gumble's Yard was a light van. We hadn't seen it down there before, and in fact it was the first sign of human activity in the neighbourhood. The driver slowed his vehicle to allow us to get the pram out of the roadway, and I had a good look at him. He had a lean, quite handsome face, and a very tiny moustache. He looked at us with some curiosity, and after we'd passed him we dawdled a little, so that he wouldn't see us crossing the open site to the Homestead. However, in a minute he had turned the corner into Hibiscus Street without showing any further interest in us, so we completed our journey.

'Did you see that fellow with the van?' I asked Dick as soon as we arrived.

'Yes, we saw him, but he didn't see us,' said Dick. 'He drove along here the way you've just come, got out of his van, and had a look in each cottage – only the ground floors, though – and then he went away again. I don't know what he was doing. Nothing at all, probably, just looking round out of curiosity, the way people do. I'm sure he didn't know about the Homestead.'

'I thought you said nobody ever came down here.'

'He's the first person I've seen,' said Dick. 'But don't look so serious. I dare say people will wander round from time to time and I wouldn't be surprised if children came here to play. It doesn't matter, so long as you keep a good lookout and make sure nobody sees you getting in and out of the Homestead.'

All the same, we decided it would be as well 36

if we didn't hang around the place any more than we could help. So when Sandra and I went to Dick's house for tea (he had got his parents to invite us, just as he promised) we took Harold and Jean with us as far as Hibiscus Street and left them playing there, with instructions not to go back to the Homestead until we came for them.

We had already planned that we would slip part of our meal into our pockets to take away for the younger ones. There were ham sandwiches and cheese sandwiches for tea, which was very convenient. But I was surprised that we were not caught. Dick was the cheekiest about it. He would take a sandwich and only pretend to bite it, and then when nobody was looking it would go straight into his pocket. Mr Hedley was never likely to notice, because he was busy telling us anecdotes beginning with 'Aye, when I were a lad. . . .' and laughing heartily at the recollection. But Mrs Hedley is a thin, shrewd person who doesn't miss much.

'Y'd think they hadn't et for a month,' she said, with a meaning look at her husband. I knew just what was in her mind. She thought Sandra and I were half starved, which in fact we weren't.

'Are your uncle and auntie in?' she asked later.

I told the same lie that I'd told before to Mrs Grimshaw. I didn't know how to avoid it. 'No,' I said, 'they've gone visiting, over at Ledford.'

'Oh,' said Mrs Hedley. 'Oh, they have, have they?' And she said no more. But when we were leaving she put a newspaper packet into Sandra's hands. And, looking quite thin-lipped and mean, as if she didn't like being caught in a kind action, she said, 'There, that's for t'little ones.' It was more food.

Well, Sandra and I felt dreadful, and Sandra said afterwards it was all she could do to avoid confessing our theft on the spot. But Dick was quite unmoved. 'That'll be breakfast for you,' he said.

'Oh, Dick,' protested Sandra, 'it doesn't feel right at all.'

'Don't worry,' said Dick. 'We'll own up to everything when it's all over. Nobody will mind then.'

'When it's all over,' said Sandra wistfully. 'Why, it's only just beginning.'

4 IT was after midnight when we began our moonlight flit. Harold and Jean were at our new home. Jean was asleep on the camp bed, covered with some of the blankets we had taken across that afternoon, but Harold was in a strange, excited state and wouldn't go to bed, although he kept yawning and rubbing his eyes. So we had given him the job of arranging everything as we brought it across from Orchid Grove. This was not really very important, but it made him feel as if he was helping.

Fred Appleby had lent his hand-cart. He didn't know what it was for, but he trusted Dick. We had left it in the back yard at Orchid Grove, and Sandra and I now walked up there to meet Dick. Dick was late, which worried us a little, but it was only because his parents had visitors and were later to bed than usual. Once they went to bed, Dick got out without any difficulty. He arrived in Orchid Grove soon after twelve, looking as fresh and cheerful as ever.

For the first journey, we loaded the handcart with the kitchen table, the fireside chair, and a few smaller belongings. Then Dick slipped out of the yard gate and along to the street corner. A low whistle told us that all was clear. Sandra and I eased the cart out into the back entry and followed him. By the time we got to the corner, Dick was whistling us on from some distance down Hibiscus Street. So again we followed, moving as quietly as possible. Luckily the Jungle is full of entries and alleyways, and there were plenty of places in which to sneak out of sight.

After a few minutes came Dick's first warning note – a higher pitched whistle. We pushed the cart into a passageway and crouched beside it. And soon we heard footsteps coming along the street. The passers-by were a couple of bus-conductors going home from the late turn, and they were fully occupied with an argument about football. United had just won the league championship, and next week Cobchester's other team, the Albion, were playing Arsenal in the Cup final.

'I tell y', Albion'll knock spots off 'em,' said one voice.

'Albion!' jeered the other. 'Blooming Albion! Couldn't knock t'skin off a rice-pudding.'

'Well, they showed Aston Villa t'way out,' said Voice One.

'Aye, and a right fluke,' said Voice Two. 'Villa should 'a' scored three times in t'second half. ...'

And the footsteps went safely past. In a minute we heard Dick's encouraging whistle, and set off

again. The next alarm came not from Dick but from behind us, when a car approached with headlamps full on. This time, as it happened, there was nowhere to take refuge. We left the cart in the road, flattened ourselves against a wall, and hoped for the best. The car driver must have seen the cart with its bulky load, but he was not curious and went straight past. And nothing more happened all the way to Gumble's Yard. There Harold let the ladder down (the things we had brought were much too bulky to go through the trapdoor) and somehow or other we manoeuvred our possessions into the Homestead.

The second journey was an awkward one because we were bringing the big double bedstead, and this was a very difficult load. We had already taken off the head and foot of the bed, and these lay on the cart quite comfortably. But the mattress and base were large, and stuck out beyond the edges of the cart in all directions. In fact we had to push the cart by pushing the bedstead, and we were afraid the whole lot might tip over at any moment. Luckily we did not meet anybody on our way, and although we had a fearful struggle to get the bedstead up the ladder we succeeded in the end. And so we went back for the third and last load, which was a fairly easy one of useful bits and pieces.

Before leaving Orchid Grove this time, we wrote a notice in block capitals and placed it prominently on the mantelpiece. It said: GONE AWAY. W. THOMPSON. This, we thought, would convince any inquirers that Walter had 'flitted' and taken his family and furniture with 42 him – not an unknown occurrence in the Jungle. We also wrote a letter to Walter, telling him where we were. This we addressed to him at the George, marking the envelope 'to be called for'. If Walter did come back, he was pretty sure to go there. I dropped the envelope through the letter-box at the George, and we set off once more for Gumble's Yard.

This time we had only got a little way down Hibiscus Street when Dick came darting back to stop us. We all stood silent, and we could hear the approach of a heavy, measured tread. Then a torch shone out, but fortunately not in our direction. 'P.C. Rawson,' said Dick in a whisper. 'Back you go, quickly!' And back we ran, meaning to turn into the nearest side-street. The rubber wheels of the cart made no noise, and our plimsolls were just as quiet, so all should have been well. But we turned the corner too quickly, and a box of crockery flew off and fell with an awful crash into the road.

'Don't stop!' hissed Dick. And Sandra and I didn't wait to argue. We sped into the side-street, cart and all. Behind, in the main road, the policeman's footsteps broke into a run, but with relief we heard them go past. Then we heard P.C. Rawson shouting something and Dick's voice answering, and we realized that Dick had stayed in the main street as a decoy. There was a pause, another shout from the policeman answered by Dick, and then running footsteps again, going away from us.

Sandra and I hurried on round the next corner, heading for Canal Street at a point lower down than the junction with Hibiscus Street. I sent

Sandra racing ahead while I followed with the cart. My heart was beating fast. Any moment I was afraid I might hear the policeman's whistle piercing the night. But in fact the sounds of pursuit had died away, and I heard nothing more.

When I reached Canal Street it was deserted and silent as usual. I hurried along it, across the bombed site and into Gumble's Yard. I still had a silly fear at every step that another policeman would suddenly appear. But there was no one. I pushed the cart into the outhouse where the standpipe was, and then I ran into the end cottage and hauled myself up through the trapdoor. Sandra was there already. But Harold had gone.

Jean was sitting up, bleary-eyed and half out of bed.

'Where's Harold?' we demanded in one voice.

Jean was only half awake. 'Harold's gone,' she said. 'He woke me up and told me. Gone home.'

'To Orchid Grove?'

'Yes, gone home. He went to fetch something.'

'How long ago?'

But Jean just gave an enormous yawn and looked blank.

'Go after him, Kevin!' said Sandra.

'Oh, help!' I said. 'I've been up there four times tonight already. And there's that bobby somewhere around.'

But there was nothing else for it. Once more I dropped down through the trapdoor and ran across the bombed site and up Canal Street. I moved stealthily but pretty fast, hoping I might catch up with Harold. And halfway along Hibiscus Street I overtook a small, determined figure.

'Harold! What are you up to?' I asked in a cross whisper. 'Didn't we tell you to stay in the Homestead?'

'I'm going to fetch something I want,' said Harold.

'What is it?'

'You'll see when I've got it,' Harold replied. There was an obstinate note in his voice.

'You can't go for it at this time of night.'

'Well, Dick said that after tonight we mustn't go to Orchid Grove any more. So I've *got* to go tonight.'

'Why didn't you ask us to bring it?'

'You wouldn't have wanted to. And you couldn't have found it, anyway.'

All the time this conversation was going on, I was glancing anxiously around. 'Now look here,' I said, 'it's too risky. We were chased by a bobby a few minutes ago. You're not going to Orchid Grove now. I won't let you.' And I gripped his arm.

'If you don't let go, I'll scream,' said Harold calmly.

I stood for a moment not knowing what to do. It dawned on me that Harold was in control of the situation.

'All right,' I said, 'but I'm coming with you. And look sharp.' And we both ran pretty fast up Hibiscus Street and into Orchid Grove. I was relieved when the door closed behind us.

'Now, let's go and get it, whatever it is,' I said. And Harold led the way up to the back bedroom that wasn't used. In the dry corner of this room there was a good deal of junk, and

Harold began rooting about among it.

'If it's a bit of spaceman stuff, I'll skin you alive,' I said.

Harold, having got his way, now looked a bit abashed.

'Well,' he said, 'it sort of is. But not in the way you think.'

He went on rummaging, and at first he couldn't find what he wanted. I stood over him, feeling crosser and crosser. And when eventually he got up, with a space helmet dangling from his hand, I nearly went through the roof.

'You little fool!' I said. 'All this for a space helmet. And anyway, you know it doesn't fit you. You threw it out months ago because it was too small.'

Suddenly Harold's eyes filled with tears.

'My dad gave it me,' he said. 'It's the only present he ever gave me.' And then he dropped the silly helmet and buried his head in my jacket, sobbing.

I stopped being cross. He really was upset. After all, it was worse for him than for me. Walter was his father, and had disappeared. I hadn't actually lost a parent myself. Still, there wasn't any point in hanging about blubbering in an empty house at two in the morning. I gave Harold half a minute to pull himself together. Then: 'Come on,' I said, 'pick up your helmet and let's get back. You'll be better when you've had some sleep.'

We were just going downstairs when the front door opened. I gave a jump. But it was only Dick.

'I gave the bobby the slip,' he said, 'but seeing

I was near here I thought it would be safer to lie low here for a while before I went home.'

Then Dick told us what had happened since he left us. As Sandra and I went off down the side-street with the hand-cart, P.C. Rawson came running up and shouted, 'What's going on here?'

Dick said, 'I just dropped my box, that's all.'

So P.C. Rawson naturally said: 'Well, what are you doing carrying boxes around at this time of night? Come over here and let's have a look at you.'

But Dick didn't mean to do that because he knew the policeman would take him home to his parents and he'd have to explain what he was up to. So he shot off in the opposite direction, with the policeman after him.

The policeman was as quick as he was, and would probably have caught him. But Dick had a few yards' start and knew every inch of the district. Round two corners he went and through an alleyway, and then he scrambled over a wall into somebody's back yard. P.C. Rawson followed into the alleyway and stood for a while only a few feet from Dick, though separated from him by the wall. He realized of course that Dick was in hiding and couldn't be far away. Then he started opening all the back-yard doors and flashing his torch inside.

Dick crouched behind a dustbin. And luckily the policeman – who was faced by a whole row of backyards, and possibly didn't feel certain that Dick was in any of them – was not very thorough. The beam of light moved past Dick's

hiding-place without stopping. Soon afterwards

the policeman seemed to give up, and went off back to Hibiscus Street. Dick waited for a while and then made his way to our house. 'There'll be nothing more heard of it,' he said confidently. 'All he'll have found is a box of old crockery, and with nothing reported missing by anybody he won't worry much about that.'

By now Dick thought it would be safe for him to set off home. Harold's mind had been taken off his troubles by Dick's story, but he was obviously tired out. I said a brief farewell to Dick – I was to meet him at the newsagent's at a quarter to seven – and Harold and I made our way, for the last time that night, to Gumble's Yard.

We didn't meet anyone, but when we got there Harold gave me the biggest surprise of all. As we passed the doorway of the first cottage in the row, Harold said in a casual way:

'That's where they put the packing-cases.'

I stopped dead.

'Where *who* put *what* packing-cases?' I demanded.

'While you were away,' said Harold. 'Some men came with a lorry and put a lot of packing-cases inside that cottage. Jean and I kept quiet, just like you said. The men didn't notice anything. They went off again quite soon.'

I went into the cottage. It was dark and I hadn't a light, so I couldn't see much. But in the corner away from the door I made out the outline of a pile of cases. Groping my way towards them, I stubbed my toe on one that must have been lying apart from the pile.

'Come on,' I said. 'Let's get out of here. And 48

Harold, don't say anything yet to Sandra about this.'

We went on to our own cottage, and I helped Harold to climb up through the trapdoor. Jean had gone back to sleep, but Sandra was still awake. She had been anxious about all three of us. I was able to tell her that Dick was all right, and that cheered her up a good deal. I didn't mention the packing-cases. I was puzzled and worried by them, but I knew Sandra had plenty on her mind already, and I wanted time to think before I said anything.

We still couldn't go to bed, because the bed stead had to be put together. To make things more awkward, we had rather a struggle with it, and got a bit cross with each other. But in the end it was done, and we made up the bed in a rough-and-ready way, too tired to care. Sandra got in at her usual end and Harold and I at the other.

Harold fell asleep at once. I didn't know about Sandra. As for myself, I knew I badly needed to sleep, but what with the strangeness of the place, and my various worries, I just couldn't Every so often a train would rumble across the viaduct, only a few yards away. Then there were the chimes of St. Jude's Church clock, sounding twice as loud at night as they did during the day. I heard the clock strike the three-quarters, then three o'clock, then a quarter past.

And then at last I fell into an uneasy sleep. I dreamed and dreamed – mostly about being chased by policemen, but once or twice about the man with the little moustache who'd seen us in Canal Street. And there was one awful

49

dream in which a policeman was confronting me with the pile of packing-cases in the end cottage and the moustached man was saying, 'He put them there.' I was protesting foolishly that I couldn't possibly have carried all those boxes when I woke up and lay awake again for quite a time. I heard the church clock chime five. Then at last I must have fallen into a deep sleep, because the next thing was that Sandra was shaking me awake and telling me that it was time to get along to Mr Mould's.

I ate a sandwich from the packet Mrs Hedley had given us, and drank some water. I peered out through all the windows to make sure that the coast was clear before going down through the trapdoor, and I looked warily around me again before I ventured into the open. It was now daylight, and as I went past the cottage at the other end of the row I had an irresistible urge to peep in. And now I had yet another shock. The packing cases – every one of them – had vanished. For a moment I wondered if I'd only dreamed of them and they'd never really been there at all. Then I felt a twinge of pain in my right foot. 'No,' I said to myself, 'you couldn't stub your toe on a dream. Those cases were there all right.' And, more puzzled than ever, I went on my way.

5 I⊤ was a damp, grey Monday morning, though
not actually raining, as I walked up Hibiscus
Street towards Mr Mould's shop. Lights were
going on, one by one, in people's houses, but
there was hardly anyone about. I met Dick at the
corner of Camellia Hill, and we went on together.
There was no mistaking the newsagent's, because
while the other shops were still shut Mr Mould's
was open and ablaze with light. Mr and Mrs
Mould and an assistant were hard at work
among piles of papers. Mr Mould was a stocky,
red-faced man who wore spectacles and was going
a bit bald. He looked as if he ought to be jovial,
but he wasn't in fact a jovial man, and this morning he looked harassed and irritable.

'This is Kevin Thompson,' Dick told him. 'I'd
like him to take over my round.'

'You'll have to see me about it later,' said Mr
Mould. 'I'm too busy just now.'

'I'd like to hand over right away,' said Dick, in a quiet but firm tone.

Mr Mould stared at him.

'Oh, you would, would you?' he said. 'It's not so easy as all that, you know.' Then the telephone rang, and there was a heated argument about a missing parcel of papers. And then the assistant asked Mr Mould to help her with some difficulty. And then a couple of early customers came in to be served. After five minutes Mr Mould returned to us, looking cross, and said:

'You can see how busy I am. Anyway, this lad can't take over on the spot. Don't you know he needs a permit from the education authority? That's the system now.'

The telephone rang again, and there was another conversation about the missing parcel. After it, Mr Mould looked crosser still.

'I don't know why you have to spring things on me like this,' he complained. 'And I don't know this lad. I don't know anything about him. Why all the hurry?'

'He needs the money,' said Dick simply.

'I can't help that,' said Mr Mould. 'He's got to have a permit. First he needs a note from his dad, and then the attendance officer has to visit him and make sure he's well clothed and shod ...' (he looked me critically up and down) '... which looks doubtful to me at the moment.'

The telephone rang again. Mr Mould spoke into it in tones of mingled annoyance and dismay.

'What? Not again? No! Oh, all right. Yes. Yes, I said! Yes; Good-bye!'

He came back to us, muttering crossly. 'I don't

know why I ever came into this business. Let you down right and left, people do. And they don't get the complaints; oh no, I get them. It isn't worth it. . . .'

He looked at us again with disfavour.

'It's only for a week or two, Mr Mould,' said Dick earnestly, 'then I can take over again. But he does need to start today.'

'Oh, all right, all right,' said Mr Mould, looking suddenly weary of the subject. 'Why should I bother? I've got enough to worry about. So far as I'm concerned, Dick, you're on a fortnight's holiday. Now look here, you – what's your name again?'

'Kevin Thompson.'

'Well, you turn up prompt at six forty-five every weekday, see. And when I say prompt I mean prompt. And you take these papers to the right address, and you put them through the letter-boxes without tearing them. And use your loaf, for heaven's sake. Some of you lads, I don't know what you're coming to. Deliver half of 'em to the wrong street, never mind the wrong house. And then the customers come in complaining again. Complain, complain, complain. . . . Oh well, if you do as well as Dick you'll be all right. You'll take him round this morning, Dick, will you?'

Dick said he would, and soon we were on our way. At first Dick had the bag of papers on his shoulder, but I told him to give it to me and he did. I never knew newspapers were so heavy. It seemed to weigh a ton. But the job was not hard at all. I soon grasped the idea, and of course as you go on delivering the load gets less and less.

We were finished within the hour. The only excitement was when somebody's dog took a dislike to me, but Dick yelled 'Gerroff!' and raised his boot, and it soon slunk off round a corner.

As we walked I told Dick about the packing-cases that had mysteriously appeared and disappeared in the end cottage. To my surprise he seemed less concerned than I had been.

'Yes, it is a bit queer,' he said, 'but you don't want to start imagining things. I expect there's some ordinary explanation. I keep telling you that you can't expect to have a monopoly of the place. After all, you don't own it, do you?'

'There were thirty or forty of those cases,' I told him. 'People don't leave things like that lying about through carelessness. It doesn't seem at all ordinary to me.'

'My guess,' said Dick, 'is that it's some lorry driver who wanted to use his lorry on the quiet for a job of his own, so he tipped his load out there for a few hours knowing it would be safe. It might be a bit shady, but I shouldn't think it was anything serious. And he wouldn't want to be seen, any more than you do. Still, it's a lesson to us to keep our eyes open all the time.'

And he seemed quite content to leave it at that. As usual, I was reassured by Dick's confidence. I changed the subject and asked him what pay I should get for delivering the papers.

'You get fifteen bob a week,' said Dick.

That seemed a lot of money to me.

'It's not so much to keep four of you fed for a week,' Dick said.

'We get free school dinners,' I pointed out.

'It's still not enough,' said Dick. He was silent 54

for a minute. Then he went on: 'I told you I had an idea about that lumber in the outhouse. We could chop it up, and make bundles of firewood to sell.'

'Would people buy it?'

'I don't see why not. They buy it in the shops, in little bundles for firelighting. And it's bulky to carry about. We'd be delivering it at the door. That would give us an advantage. I reckon it's worth trying.'

'All right,' I said. Actually I thought it was a very good idea, but I couldn't feel a lot of enthusiasm just then because I was very tired. I found myself looking forward to getting to school and sitting down at my desk. And when I did arrive there it was a constant struggle not to fall asleep in class. Even Miss Woodrow, who teaches us English and takes a special interest in me because I'm rather good at it, began to get impatient with me for not attending properly. As for Mr Jones, the geography master, who always enjoys scoring off the boys when he gets a chance, well, I came in for some heavy sarcasm from him. At dinner-time I knew I ought to have as good a meal as possible, but I hadn't any appetite and couldn't eat much. In the afternoon I was still tired but I managed to pull myself together a bit more, and I was relieved to get through without serious trouble.

After Dick had had his tea he came round to Gumble's Yard again, and this time he brought an axe and we set to work to chop up some of the wood from the outhouse. We cut it into quite small chips, and Sandra helped us to fasten them into neat bundles.

'We can sell them at a penny a bundle,' I said.

'Twopence,' said Sandra firmly. 'That's what they charge in the shops, and we're delivering them free.'

'Tough as old boots, aren't you?' said Dick.

'Somebody's got to have their head screwed on right,' retorted Sandra. She looked more like my mother than ever. Mother had been dead for three years, but I remembered her well. She'd had a hard life, and watched her pennies like a hawk. Sandra is well set for the same life. She'll never be a romantic girl, but after all there isn't much romance in the Jungle. She'll know which shop to buy her potatoes at, and that's more important.

When we had finished, we stacked the bundles of firewood in the old pram – the hand-cart had gone back to Fred Appleby – but it was getting dark and we decided not to start selling them that night. We couldn't rest, though, because there was still a lot to be done in the Homestead. We spent another hour hard at work, driving in nails and hooks, putting up a shelf, organizing our various possessions, and then tidying up once more. And when we'd finished I must say the place could hardly be recognized as the bare, depressing, cobwebby attic it had been when we first saw it.

We'd left the windows dirty deliberately, because we didn't want the place to look inhabited. But we'd put thick curtains up, to be drawn in the evening so that nobody from outside would see a light, and they made things more homely as well. In the middle of the floor was the paraffin stove, and in front of it one of the rugs. A 56 couple of candles stood in their holders on boxes at opposite sides of the room. Sandra and Dick and I, being the oldest, had the chairs. Harold and Jean sat on the edge of the bed. The table had been pushed against one of the walls, and above it hung two or three pans, clean and gleaming. (You couldn't exactly cook on the paraffin stove, but you could warm things up quite well if you stood a pan on top of it.) The general effect was not luxurious, but it was really quite cosy, and the great thing about the Homestead was that it was absolutely spotless, which was more than you could ever have said of 40 Orchid Grove.

'I like it here,' declared Jean. 'I'm not going back to an ordinary house. I shall live here for ever. And when I'm married I'll bring my husband here, and all our children, and we'll have some dogs . . . .' She was quite happy. Harold on the other hand sat silently brooding. I was a bit worried about Harold, but I had so many other things on my mind that I hadn't really given him any proper thought.

'Tell us a story, Kevin,' said Sandra, as she had done at Orchid Grove two nights before. That seemed a good way of cheering Harold up, as well as keeping everybody entertained. This time I made it a space story, and I put everything I'd got into it. It was one of the best stories I ever told. I was glad to see Harold becoming absorbed, and after a while he began putting me right on the technical details, which always makes him feel pleased with himself. I felt better too, and was able for a while to forget our problems. Telling a story always gives me confidence. It makes me feel I'm in control of events, and can make things come right.

This feeling lasted until after I'd finished and Dick had gone home and we were all in bed. We'd had three very strange days, I reflected, but here we were safe and sound together, and all would be well in the end. We'd sell the firewood tomorrow evening, so as to have a bit of money in hand, and if we were still on our own by the week-end I would somehow get over to Ledford and find Uncle Bob, and he would sort out our difficulties.

My cheerful mood was disturbed a little when I heard a subdued sound from Harold, lying beside me, and realized that it was a sob. I whispered to him softly:

'Don't worry, Harold, your dad'll come back.'

I hadn't particularly intended to say that, but the words seemed the only ones that would be comforting. Poor kid, I thought, I wonder if his dad ever will.

I heard St. Jude's clock strike ten, but not the quarter, for tiredness came over me again in a great wave, and I fell fast asleep.

6

THE next day, Tuesday, was a quiet day, at least until after tea, and I hadn't an inkling of how events were going to gather speed. I managed the newspaper round quite well on my own, and as I'd had a better night's sleep I didn't feel so bad in school as the day before. I still hadn't any appetite for dinner, though. In the evening Dick came round again and we set off to sell our bundles of firewood. We didn't go to the Jungle, where too many people knew us and we might have been asked awkward questions. Instead we went to the other side of Camellia Hill (locally it's just called the Hill) which is in St. Jude's parish. It's the same sort of district as the Jungle, but the streets all have girls' names – old-fashioned ones, like Gertrude Street and Emily Street and Ada Street.

We did quite well. It was only at about every sixth house that we actually sold any firewood, but when we did we generally sold at least half a dozen bundles. After an hour or so we had over six shillings and were feeling quite pleased with ourselves.

Then we met Tom Tupper and his gang. These were some of the boys we used to fight with regularly at one time. They used to come marauding in the Jungle, and of course we couldn't stand for that. But lately we hadn't seen much of them. However, we were on their territory.

'Jungle apes! Jungle apes!' they shouted at us.

We took no notice at first. We wanted to go on selling our firewood. But they kept shouting at us, and finally one of them dashed up and pushed the pram over. Our bundles of chips flew into the roadway.

I bent down to pick them up. I would still have liked to avoid a fight. But Dick was furious.

'The next who comes will get his block knocked off!' he shouted.

This was a mistake. There were six of them to two of us. And they soon closed in. In a minute there was a fine scrap in progress. Dick laid into them right and left and gave one or two of them something to think about. Tom Tupper got a lovely clip on the ear. I'm not the fighter Dick is, but I did my best and lashed out in all directions. However we were overwhelmed and soon we were both on the ground, with the St. Jude's lot milling round and shoving each other out of the way in order to get a swipe at us. Things didn't look too good.

Fortunately a fight never goes on for long in the streets. Somebody comes and stops it. And in this case the person who came along was the new curate of St Jude's.

The curate of St Jude's is the Reverend Anthony Boyd. Dick knew him already, but I had never seen him before. He's tall and thin and wears glasses. But he isn't soft – far from it. Tom and the louts didn't wait to get the sharp edge of his tongue. They were off before he got to the spot. Dick picked himself up, red-faced and furious, and looked as if he was going to set off after them, but thought better of it. I was slower; I'd had a nasty thump in the stomach. Mr Boyd helped me to get up and brush myself down. Then all three of us picked up bundles of firewood and put them back in the pram.

'What was that about?' asked Mr Boyd.

'Oh, nothing, really,' said Dick. 'We come from the other side of the Hill, you know.'

Mr Boyd understood that sort of thing quite well. He didn't ask any more about the fight.

'How's business?' he said.

'Not so bad,' said Dick in an offhand tone. I said nothing.

Mr Boyd looked at me curiously. I could tell he was comparing my appearance with Dick's. Dick is well-built and healthy-looking and has good stout clothes. I'm quite healthy myself as a matter of fact, but I am skinny at the best of times, and I knew I looked pale and tired. And my clothes were not too good. I avoided his eye.

'What do you want money for?' he inquired.

Again I said nothing, but Dick replied rapidly, 'We want to buy an airgun.'

Mr Boyd looked more curiously still at me. 'Do you want an airgun too?' he inquired.

'Yes, sir,' I said.

'It looks to me,' said Mr Boyd, 'as if there are things you need more than that. Let's see your shoes.'

I was still wearing the plimsolls I'd worn for the moonlight flit, and in fact they were the only shoes I had. Also, they'd a hole in the sole. Mr Boyd grimaced.

'What street do you live in?' he asked sharply.

I said, 'Orchid Grove,' because I'd lost my presence of mind and couldn't think of anything else to say.

'That's not far away,' said Mr Boyd. 'I think I'll come home with you, if you don't mind. I'd like to have a word with your father.'

'He hasn't got a father,' said Dick.

'Or with your mother,' said Mr Boyd.

'He hasn't got a mother.'

'Well, anyway,' said Mr Boyd, 'I feel sure a good deal could be done for you. I'd like to find something out about your background.'

He set off in the direction of the Jungle. For a minute or two we trailed along with him. I did not know what to do. Then:

'Please, sir,' said Dick, 'we're in a jam. Could we have a talk to you privately before we go on to Kevin's house?'

Mr Boyd halted and considered this for a moment.

'All right,' he said. 'Come to my digs.'

So we turned another way, and in a minute or two we arrived at Mr Boyd's lodgings, which were round the corner from St Jude's Church. It was the ground floor of an old house that had probably once been rather smart before all the 62 streets were built round it. Mr Boyd's sitting-room was large and shabby, but comfortable-looking.

A young lady got up from an armchair as we went in. When she turned towards us I had a surprise. It was Miss Woodrow, who taught me English at school. And straightway I had a second surprise, because Mr Boyd went over and kissed her, right in front of us. This is not what you expect to happen to schoolteachers. It struck me, as it never had done at school, that Miss Woodrow was pretty.

'My fiancée,' explained Mr Boyd. He wasn't at all embarrassed.

'Well, I know Kevin,' said Miss Woodrow. She smiled at me in a friendly way, and then turned to Dick. 'I know you quite well, too, by sight,' she said, 'but I don't think I've ever taught you.'

'I'm Dick Hedley,' said Dick.

'Oh yes, I remember now. The right-wing wizard.' This was a reference to Dick's ability as a footballer. He reddened, but I knew he was quite pleased really.

'Dick Hedley,' repeated Mr Boyd, as if he was fixing us firmly in his mind, 'and Kevin – what's your other name?'

'Thompson.'

'Right. Now, is your business too private for Miss Woodrow to hear?'

Dick and I looked at each other. 'I don't think it matters,' said Dick. 'But please will you promise not to tell this to anybody?'

Mr Boyd looked doubtful. 'I don't know,' he said. 'It might be my duty, you know.' But he
63 went on: 'I won't tell anybody if it's at all reason-

able not to do so.' And that was the most we could get from him. As there was really not much choice, Dick went ahead and told them our story.

When he had finished, Mr Boyd looked grave.

'You must realize,' he said, 'that this isn't the sort of thing I can keep quiet. But I think you're all jolly brave. You're wrong, but you've got the right stuff in you.'

I hadn't said anything up to now. But now I spoke up.

'Please, Mr Boyd –' I said.

'You can call me Tony,' said Mr Boyd. 'I have a feeling I shall be seeing quite a lot more of you. We might as well be friends.'

I couldn't call him Tony, at least not then, because I was too shy, but actually he and Miss Woodrow did later become great friends of ours, and as I always think of them as Tony and Sheila I shall call them that in writing this account.

'I'd like Sandra and Harold and Jean and me to stay together until I can get my Uncle Bob over from Ledford,' I said. 'Then he'll make sure we're all right. He's a really good sort. Don't let them take us away – please don't – until he's been.'

'They'll be all right,' said Dick, putting on his most confident tone. 'I'll look after them myself.'

Tony looked even more doubtful.

'There's really only one thing we can do, isn't there, Sheila?' he said.

'I'm afraid so,' said Sheila. 'But don't you think we ought to go and see them in this place of theirs before we do anything else?'

Everyone thought this was a good idea.

'We'll have some supper before we go,' Sheila added, 'and perhaps we can take something along for the other children.'

She put on an apron and went into Tony's tiny kitchen, and before long there was a wonderful smell of frying bacon. It brought my appetite straight back. I hadn't eaten properly for days, and I suddenly realized I was terrifically hungry. The smell sort of floated in and filled my whole consciousness.

Tony hovered between the kitchen and the room where we were. Sheila was looking very pretty in her apron with a lock of hair falling over her eyes. Dick, who has a romantic side, nudged me and sang under his breath a snatch of song about 'head over heels in love'. But I couldn't really take my mind off the food. And in a few minutes we were all eating heartily. Then Sheila started making sandwiches. 'You'll be on short rations for a week, Tony,' she said. 'But it's in a good cause.'

We set off on foot for Gumble's Yard. Nobody was around, and we all negotiated the trapdoor successfully. Sandra was just putting the younger children to bed. Of course they were excited at seeing strangers. They had had a bit of supper, but they were still hungry, and they and Sandra sat round and wolfed all the sandwiches.

Sheila made a tour of inspection and was quite impressed by our arrangements. She looked at Sandra with respect.

'So you really look after this place, and the two children, and go to school as well?' she asked.

'Of course. Who else?' said Sandra shortly.

'Well, I think it's wonderful. I don't know how you manage.'

'Surprising what you can do when you have to,' said Sandra. It sounded just like my mother talking. She had never been one for compliments either.

'Is there anything I can do to help?'

'I'm quite all right, thank you,' said Sandra, in the tone of one who didn't see much point in continuing the conversation. I thought she must sound rather rude, but I know just how Sandra's mind works, and I decided I would try to explain to Sheila later. You see, Sandra takes pride in being very self-reliant, and she's inclined to take an offer of help as suggesting that she can't quite cope on her own. It can be very difficult.

Anyway, Tony and Sheila stayed for about half an hour, but it was obvious that the younger children wouldn't go to sleep as long as they were there, so we left Sandra in charge again, and Dick and I and the grown-ups strolled around outside. Tony looked rather worried when he saw that the canal bank was only a few yards away, but we assured him that Harold and Jean were well enough trained to look after themselves.

'Well,' Tony said after a few minutes, 'I don't think I've any right to leave you fending for yourselves like that.'

My heart sank.

'But,' he went on, 'there's just the possibility that the couple who were looking after you might come back of their own accord in a day or two. If that happened, it would certainly help to keep things going if we could avoid reporting them. 66

And then there's this uncle of yours. Tell me some more about him.'

So I told them about Uncle Bob in Ledford. He is a real uncle – the brother of Walter and my father – but he couldn't take us into his home after mother died because he has a crippled wife to look after. He doesn't earn high wages, being only a semi-skilled worker, but he used to send money to Walter to help in looking after us, and once I had been to stay with him.

'I don't know if he'll be able to do much for you,' said Tony thoughtfully, 'but he certainly ought to be consulted, whatever happens. I'll tell you what we'll do. Today is Tuesday. Sheila and I will help you to carry on for another day or two if we can. As I said, the people who walked out on you may have walked back by then, and in any case I'd like to talk to your uncle before I do anything more. But if you're not satisfactorily fixed up by the week-end – really fixed up, I mean – that will be the end. We shall have to do what's in your own best interest.'

I knew he was stretching a point to go even as far as that. In any case we were in no position to argue.

'Have you got your uncle's address?' Tony went on.

Unfortunately I hadn't. I knew Walter was still hearing from him until a week or two previously, but naturally I never looked at the letters, and it was three or four years since I'd been there.

'No,' I said. 'But I can find the house.'

'Sure?'

'Absolutely sure,' I said.

'We'll go over there tomorrow evening, you and I,' said Tony. 'Come round to my digs straight after school. If we get a move on we'll catch the five o'clock train.' He turned to Sheila. 'You'll keep an eye on the others, won't you?'

'She needn't bother,' said Dick in his lordliest tone. 'I'll see that they're all right.' He and Sandra are a real pair, I thought. They know it all, between them.

Sheila just smiled, but I knew she would consider herself on duty, and I was relieved.

'Five o'clock train from Cobchester Central, then,' said Tony briskly as we said our good-byes.

We had wandered some distance towards Hibiscus Street, so Dick and I had to walk back along Canal Street to get to the Homestead. Halfway there we were overtaken by a heavy lorry, going pretty fast. We were startled. It was the first vehicle we had seen down here since the light van two days before. We watched with mounting alarm as the lorry pulled up, with a crunch of tyres upon cinder, on the vacant ground in front of Gumble's Yard.

Instinctively Dick and I ducked behind a low wall. And peeping out we saw two men jump down from the lorry and start unloading packing-cases at a great pace.

Some thirty or forty cases were unloaded. From a distance they looked just like the ones I'd seen the other night. Then the two men began humping them from the ground into the end cottage where the others had been. They worked with enormous haste. The pile of cases dwindled. When the last one had disappeared, the two men leapt back into the lorry. Dick and I shrank 68 further into cover. The engine roared, and in a moment the lorry was heading past us up Canal Street at a remarkable speed for so large a vehicle.

Dick and I stared at each other. We hadn't mentioned the packing-case mystery to Tony – partly because we'd thought it might make him less likely to allow us to stay, and partly because we'd managed to convince ourselves that it wasn't really important.

'I expect they'll disappear again overnight, like the others,' said Dick. He spoke a little uneasily. 'We must just be extra careful, that's all.'

'But . . .' I began.

We each knew what the other was thinking. After the furtive haste of the operation we'd just watched, we felt sure that something illegal and at the same time highly organized was going on.

'Let's go in and have a good look at those cases!' urged Dick.

I agreed reluctantly. I knew there was danger. And a further thought was worrying me. Though the two men were some distance away, I thought I had recognized them. One, I was sure, was the man with the tiny moustache who had driven the light van up Canal Street on the day we arrived. And the other had a still more familiar appearance. He looked remarkably like Walter.

7 By the light of a stub of candle, Dick and I examined the pile of packing-cases. It wasn't a neat pile. The cases had been hastily and roughly stacked, and as before there were one or two that lay apart from the rest.

All of them were stout and were fastened with steel bands.

'We can't get into them,' I said. 'Anyway, let's go. I don't like it in here.'

'I wonder if they know how many cases there are,' said Dick thoughtfully.

'Well, they didn't seem to be counting them,' I said. 'They were just hustling them in here as fast as they could.'

'Let's take one up to the Homestead,' suggested Dick.

I was alarmed. 'A bit risky, isn't it?' I said. 'Suppose they come back and catch us? Or even if we manage it, suppose they count the cases when they come to collect them, and realize there's one missing? Then they might start nosing around. . . .'

I shuddered. Standing there in the dank, doorless hovel, and remembering once more that we were far from any inhabited place but only a few yards from the canal, I felt frightened. Above us were Sandra and the two younger children. I didn't want anything to happen to them. At the moment I was bitterly sorry we had ever come to Gumble's Yard, and I certainly hadn't any wish to get involved in the affair of the packing-cases.

'Anyway,' I went on, 'if we took one upstairs, we'd have to tell Sandra what it was all about. And I bet she'd refuse to have it there.'

'That's true,' admitted Dick. As I was speaking, he had been walking round the pile of cases, examining each in turn by the light of the candle, and now he said with interest, 'There's one here that's marked with a cross in red pencil.'

'Well, what if there is?'

'It might just mean something,' said Dick. 'Look, Kevin, you're right about not taking any of these into the Homestead. It's too risky. But let's put this case with the red mark apart from the rest, and put a bit of the rubbish from the floor on top of it – not hiding it exactly, but so that if they were in a hurry they might miss it.'

'All right,' I said reluctantly. I would have preferred not to touch anything, but I could tell that Dick was determined. So we moved the marked case towards the back of the room and half-concealed it with some newspapers.

'There!' said Dick with satisfaction. 'It's not hidden enough to make them suspicious, but if they came in the darkness they could easily leave it behind. Then we'd find out what all this is about.'

I didn't care what it was all about, but I felt increasingly apprehensive, and after Dick had gone home and we'd all gone to bed I went on worrying. At one point I made up my mind to tell Sandra everything, and was about to wake her up, but I heard her soft breathing and hadn't the heart to disturb her. In the end I fell into a nervous sleep, from which I awoke several times in the dark and found myself listening intently for noises from down below.

It must have been the fifth or sixth time of waking when I did hear a sound – not from below, however, but from the canal. Whether it was this that had disturbed me I didn't know, for it was not very loud – just a gentle chug-chug approaching along the water. I got up quietly and went over to the window. It was dawn, and in the grey light I could distinguish the outline of a motor-barge. The engine stopped, the barge drew alongside the wharf and a man jumped ashore and tied up. This time there was no doubt at all who it was. Walter. A second man followed, and I was pretty sure it was the man with the moustache. A third man stayed on board the barge – a big, brawny fellow I hadn't seen before.

Walter and the second man, again working at the headlong pace that had so impressed me the night before, began manhandling the cases from the end cottage down to the quay. They tipped them down to the brawny man in the barge who, with amazing strength, caught them and stowed them away. From time to time he swore viciously at one or the other of his companions for not tipping a case exactly as it was wanted. Otherwise nobody spoke. That would be a nasty man to come up against in a brawl, I thought.

In a few minutes the work was done. The big man started the engine, Walter and his mate untied the barge and leaped aboard, and they chugged quietly back the way they had come. They were soon out of sight round a bend.

I was relieved to see them go. I didn't know whether they'd taken the marked case or not, but I rather hoped they had. Anyway, it was now obvious that the previous load of cases, two nights before, must have gone the same way. What worried me was that it looked as though this was a regular procedure, and if so there was an obvious danger that one or more of the men might arrive at the wrong moment and catch us entering or leaving the Homestead. And then what would happen?

I was still pondering the subject when St Jude's clock struck six. This was my time for getting up. Sandra stirred – she is as reliable as an alarm clock – and looked round, but seeing that I was awake and out of bed she turned over and settled down again. I washed myself skimpily in a basin of cold water, got dressed, and ate the sandwich that Sandra had put out for me the night before. Then, as quietly as possible so as not to disturb anyone, I lowered myself through the trapdoor.

I had made up my mind that I wouldn't even 74

look in the end cottage. But when it came to the point I couldn't resist peering round the doorway. The light was poor inside, and at first glance I thought the marked case was gone with the rest. But that was only because our camouflage had been effective. On closer inspection I saw that it was still there. It gave me an uneasy feeling, as if we'd had a time-bomb in our midst. I found myself wishing heartily that Dick wouldn't meddle with things that didn't concern him. With some misgivings I went on my way to Mr Mould's.

That day I knew for the first time what it was to be really exhausted. My previous tiredness had been nothing in comparison. I had had three very active days without a good night's sleep. I managed all right with the newspaper round, although it seemed longer and the weight seemed heavier than before. In school I got through the morning fairly well, mainly because we had woodwork and gym, which kept me on the move. But this was only adding to my tiredness. After dinner it was hopeless. To make matters worse, we had geography, with Mr Jones. He rather fancies himself, being an ex-officer, and probably thinks he ought to be teaching in a public school instead of Camellia Hill Modern. He speaks a bit la-di-da, and likes to make a boy look silly so that he himself can look clever by comparison. We all have him weighed up. A man like that can be nasty if he likes, so I tried desperately hard to pay attention.

But it was a losing fight. Before long I slid into a doze. Then I had an uneasy dream that the men I'd seen were forcing their way into the

Homestead and demanding the return of their packing-case.

'Keep out! Keep out!' I shouted. And I jolted awake to find the whole class staring at me.

Mr Jones, who had been at the blackboard, tossed his chalk gently from hand to hand and watched me quizzically. There was quite a pause. Then:

'I hope I haven't been disturbing your slumbers, Thompson.'

Everybody tittered. I went red.

'Of course, we all know that geography is less important than catching up on your night's sleep, after television or whatever it was.'

Everybody tittered again. Mr Jones was enjoying himself. He looked at me benevolently and threw his chalk from hand to hand a few more times.

'Perhaps you could do with a little more rest than my inconsiderate talking seems to permit,' he said at length. 'I think, Thompson, you had better stay behind after school, and relax for another half-hour while I mark some papers.'

The class all laughed again, but I was horrified. How was I to meet Tony as we had arranged.

'Please, sir,' I burst out, 'I have to meet somebody....'

'Oh, you have, Thompson?' Mr Jones was affable. 'Well, now, let's see, what had we better do?' He pretended to think for a moment. 'Well, you know,' he said at length, 'I think that person – I won't ask whether it's he or she – will just have to wait.'

There were more titters from the class, and I 76

knew it was no good arguing. That would only provide Mr Jones with more opportunities for getting a cheap laugh. When school ended, I pretended to have forgotten, and began to file out with the others, but Mr Jones fixed me with an eye and I returned to my place. I hadn't even had a chance to send a message.

With nobody watching, Mr Jones didn't bother to continue his act. He told me sharply to get on reading a chapter of the textbook, and he sat silently marking his papers. He kept me for the exact half-hour. Then he said curtly:

'You can go now, Thompson. Another time, stay awake.'

I shot off, and hurried round to Tony's lodgings. The door was open, but there was nobody there. I called his name aloud and flung open all the inner doors. No Tony. Perhaps he'd gone down to Gumble's Yard for me, I thought, and at once I ran out again, and down towards Canal Street. As I approached the cottages I looked round warily, in case Walter or his associates should be there, but there was no sign of life. I went inside and swung myself up through the trapdoor. And then I had the biggest shock of all. The Homestead was empty. No Sandra, no Harold, no Jean. Yet the table was laid for tea. There was a pile of bread and butter already cut, and the tea-pot had been put on the oil-stove to warm.

Sick with anxiety, I sank down on the bed. Everything seemed to be going to pieces. I told myself that there were a dozen reasons why
Sandra and the children might have gone out.

And yet I was not satisfied. Had the gang been again and found them? That was the most alarming and, I feared, the most likely explanation. Yet somehow it didn't quite seem to fit. Could these men have spirited Sandra and the children away so quickly and neatly, leaving everything in apple-pie order and the table still laid for tea? It didn't seem probable.

I was still wondering what had happened when the trapdoor began to open again. My heart thumped. But it was only Dick.

'Where's everyone?' he asked, surprised.

'I don't know,' I said wildly. 'I just don't know. Dick, I'm scared stiff. We ought never to have started all this. I was kept in and missed Tony, and now they've all disappeared.'

In fact I was getting rather overwrought. In spite of my reasoning, my imagination began to get on top of me. I pictured Sandra and the children bound and gagged in the bottom of that barge; I pictured the place surrounded by dubious characters who might even now be creeping up on us. . . .

'Calm down, Kevin,' said Dick. 'Let's put two and two together.'

'It's all very well for you –' I began, but Dick interrupted me.

'Listen,' he said. 'First, you missed Tony. Second, Sandra and the others have disappeared. Now apart from us, Tony and Sheila are the only people who know about the Homestead. Don't you think the two things are most likely connected? When you didn't turn up, Tony must have collected the others and taken them somewhere.'

78

'But I've come straight from his lodgings and I didn't see them.'

'Tony's a quick worker,' said Dick. 'And he needn't necessarily have taken them to his lodgings.'

'You mean . . . the police? Or the Cruelty?'

Dick nodded.

'Oh, he wouldn't!' I cried. 'Not so suddenly and without telling us.'

'He might,' said Dick.

'But it wouldn't be fair, after what he said.'

'Remember,' said Dick, 'he's a clergyman. He must feel he has to do his duty. He was giving you one chance, and he thinks you haven't taken it. I don't see how you can blame him if he's decided to bring the whole thing into the open.'

'If he's done that,' I said, 'the game's up. We're finished.' And although the previous night I had been regretting the move to Gumble's Yard a lump came in my throat. At least we had all been together there.

Dick looked grave.

'It certainly seems to be a crisis,' he said. 'You know what, Kevin? You must get over to Ledford on your own, tonight. Find your Uncle Bob. That's the last hope. If he won't do anything for you, you've had it anyway. But if there's a chance that he could take you in, then it will be better for you to appeal to him yourself, rather than have the authorities approaching him with all four of you already in a home.'

That seemed to make sense. But I was not entirely convinced by Dick's explanation of events.

It didn't seem in keeping with Tony's character

as I saw it. I told Dick about the morning visit of the barge, and then about my fears that the children had been kidnapped.

'I don't think so for a moment,' said Dick with conviction. 'I dare say those fellows are crooks. But kidnap three children? – not on your life. If they'd found them, they'd probably kick them out and threaten them with a tanning if they went near the place again. No, I'm sure mine's the right explanation. Take my advice and go. The best thing you can do is to get to Ledford on the next train.'

'I've no money,' I said.

'I've got enough for the single fare,' said Dick, 'and I was looking up the trains last night. You've missed the five o'clock train that you and Tony would have got. The next is 6.15. It gets there just after half past seven. Will it take you long to find your uncle's house?'

'Not long,' I said confidently. 'Twenty minutes' walk, perhaps. Less than that on the tram. But, of course, he might not be in.'

'Well, find him anyway and bring him across tonight,' said Dick in his most commanding tone. 'Take him to Tony's digs, whatever time it is. In the meantime I'll take charge at this end. Don't worry about the others. I'm sure they'll be all right.'

As he finished speaking, St Jude's clock struck the quarter. Quarter past five.

'You needn't set off for another half-hour,' said Dick, 'and you might as well stay here until then, in case any of our missing people turn up.'

'All right,' I said. I slumped wearily on the 80

bed, and in a minute I would have been asleep, in spite of all my worries.

'Hold on,' said Dick, 'I want you to help me with that packing-case.'

I jerked up again.

'Oh, leave it alone, Dick,' I urged him. 'We're far better having nothing to do with that.'

'I don't agree,' said Dick sharply. 'Maybe I'm wrong, but I've a feeling that this business may affect your future a good deal. You said you were sure Walter was one of the men, didn't you?'

'Yes, but . . .'

'Well, then, you want to know what he's up to. Come along, Kevin, it won't take long.'

We went round to the end cottage. The packing-case with the red-pencil cross was still there.

'Let's take it up to the Homestead,' said Dick, 'so we can open it in peace.'

I opened my mouth to argue, and then closed it again. With a good deal of difficulty we manoeuvred the case through the trapdoor. Dick had brought pliers and a chisel, and had collected from the outhouse the axe that we'd used to chop up the firewood. My heart thumped yet again as we removed the steel bands and broke the case open.

I don't know quite what I expected to see inside. But what I did see was certainly nothing that I would ever have guessed. Inside the case were a couple of dozen neat, identical cardboard boxes. And inside each cardboard box was an electric iron. An ordinary electric iron, brand new.

Dick and I stared at each other.

'Electric irons,' said Dick thoughtfully. 'Electric irons. . . .'

'Yes, I can see they're electric irons,' I said. 'But why? What are they doing here? What . . . ?'

'Oh, I don't know!' snapped Dick. 'Get on your way. You'll be missing that train.'

8   THE train rattled its way across the Pennines into Yorkshire. I sat in a corner seat, feeling glum and anxious. For one thing, I felt as if I was moving away from the centre of events. I wished I knew what was going on in Cobchester behind me. What had happened to Sandra, and Harold, and Jean? What had happened to Tony? What were the men up to who had shipped the packing-cases on to the barge? (I still shuddered as I recalled the brutal face of the big fellow who had caught and stowed them.) What was Walter doing among such a crew? Why did the cases contain – of all things – electric irons? Had Dick a plan of action, and if so what was it? The whole thing had got quite beyond me.

I had to admit to myself that there was nothing I could have done in Cobchester that Dick could not do equally well; also my present task – to find our only known relative – was an
85 important one that nobody but myself could

carry out. But here I had a fresh anxiety to trouble me. For although I had spoken confidently enough when Tony asked me if I could be sure of finding my uncle – and indeed I had felt confident at the time – I now began to wonder whether it would be as straightforward as I had expected. I knew the name of the district, I knew which main road the trams took from the city centre, I could recall quite clearly the road junction where we used to get off the tram. And from there I thought I could still weave my way through the streets to where Uncle Bob lived. And yet ... it was four years since I had been there. I'd only been just nine years old at the time. Supposing I didn't remember as well as I thought? Suppose I finished by wandering hopelessly round, lost and penniless, unable even to get back to Cobchester?

On the opposite seat was an evening paper that somebody had left behind. To take my mind off my worries I glanced through it. But there was nothing really interesting. There were the comings and goings for some big international conference, with photographs of various blank important faces. Nearer home, 'baby-faced Flick Williams' had broken out of Cobchester Gaol. For a moment that seemed to stir some recollection in my mind, but I couldn't quite place it. And the Albion team was announced for next week-end's Cup Final, but that didn't excite me, because I supported United and anyway it was time to be thinking of cricket now. I threw the paper down and stared out of the window, my thoughts returning willy-nilly to the old track.

I was still worrying when the train pulled in to Ledford station, but I felt better when I was on my own feet again and doing something. Going from the station I soon found the tram-stop. I had a few coppers, but I decided not to take the tram, because I didn't know what stop to ask for, and I had a dread of arousing suspicion. But I followed the lines, and was soon trudging along the main road, remembering landmarks as I went. So far so good.

Over the bridge with the black waters of the Ledder river beneath; yes, I remembered that. Past Pollards' engineering works; yes, that was right. Then the Bethesda Chapel, sooty as ever. I was doing splendidly. I had a moment's doubt when I came to the junction of two main roads; which should I take? But far along one of them I recognized the sign of the strangely named pub, the Bear and Pineapple, where I remembered that Uncle Bob used to have an occasional glass of beer. And beside the Bear and Pineapple, when I reached it, I recognized the sloping side-street we used to walk down from Uncle's house.

Up the slope I went. I felt confident now. At the top was a bare patch of ground; now a row of posts and the entrance to an alleyway that led to a parallel street. I had only to go to the end and turn right and I would see my uncle's house. I knew I was right. There was no possibility of mistake. I almost ran along that last street, and rounded the final corner. And then I gasped with dismay. Instead of the row of houses where my uncle had lived, there was only a bare, black cindery site, with a few oddments of rubbish on it. The entire row had been demolished.

I sank down hopelessly on an old box on the empty site. I felt suddenly deflated. With the loss of the hope that had buoyed me up I remembered that I was tired and hot and thirsty. I was also without any money to get me back to Cobchester.

For a few minutes I sat slumped with my head in my hands. Then an old woman came past.

'What's up, love?' she asked me.

'I was looking for my uncle,' I said. 'Bob Thompson.'

'Yer sittin' right where his house was. That'd be his kitchen, where you are. I'd be in t'front room, if house was here. Aye, I knew Bob Thompson all right. He were a good neighbour o' mine. But he's gone; gone a year back.'

'Do you know where?' I asked.

The old crone shook her head. 'Nay, lad,' she said, 'I'm seventy-nine. I've enough to do lookin' after myself, wi'out worritin' over neighbours' business. Why don't you ask at t'shop at t'corner there?'

That was sensible. I went over to the corner shop. Joseph Harrison, it said over the door. It was the kind of shop we have in the Jungle, too: the kind that is open at all hours and sells everything. In the window was a jumble of sweet-bottles, dummy cigarette-packets, magazines, penholders on cards, shoelaces, and just plain junk. Mr Joseph Harrison, a big, red-faced man in shirtsleeves, came forward at a leisurely pace from the back of the shop.

'Well, lad?' he said.

'I was looking for my uncle,' I said once more. 88

'His name's Bob Thompson. I believe he's gone from here.'

'Aye,' said Mr Harrison. 'Aye, he has that. Went about a year ago, when they pulled yon houses down.' He gave me a long, slow look. 'Are y'on your own, lad?'

'Yes,' I said. I took a deep breath and lied. 'My parents sent me over to look for him. They'd lost touch; hadn't heard from him for quite a while.'

'Oh,' said Mr Harrison. There was a moment's pause while he thought things out. Then he turned towards the back and called, in a voice that made me jump, 'Mike!'

Nothing happened.

Mr Harrison went to the inner door and roared like a bull. 'Mike!'

A fair, curly-haired young man of perhaps eighteen, wearing a boiler-suit, appeared from the back.

'I was in the yard, Dad,' he said, 'cleaning the bike.'

'Cleanin' t'bike!' said Mr Harrison. 'You cleaned it yesterday. And t'day before an' all. You'll be takin' it to bed with you next. Now, Mike, where did folk go who lived in Hanson Terrace? This lad's looking for Bob Thompson.'

'They went to Scarsholme Estate,' said Mike promptly.

'Scarsholme's a big place,' said Mr Harrison. 'Do you know what part?'

'No,' said Mike. 'No, I don't. Could be anywhere.' He edged towards the back again.

'Wait a minute, wait a minute,' said Mr Harrison. 'Your bike won't run away.'

He turned to me again. It looked as though Mr Harrison, though not a quick thinker, was a determined one.

'Now, lad,' he said, 'what's your name, by the way?'

'Kevin,' I told him. 'Kevin Thompson.'

'Well, Kevin, there's two ways you could find out. You could ask at t'Housing Department, but they'll be closed now. You'd have to leave it until tomorrow.'

'I can't,' I said. 'I've nowhere to stay tonight.'

'The other way is this. Your uncle was a bowls player, a right good one. Wherever he is now, I reckon he'll still be playing bowls. Now, is that lad of mine still listening? Mike, I want you to take Kevin up on your motor-bike to the City Arms at Scarsholme Corner. They have a big bowling club there. Maybe Bob Thompson plays there, or if he doesn't he may have played against them and somebody'll know him.'

Mike's face had brightened at the mention of his motor-bike. 'I'll take him,' he said. 'You see, Dad, didn't I tell you a bike's a useful thing? I'll take him with pleasure. Come on, Kevin, are you ready?'

Mr Harrison raised a ponderous hand, like a policeman on point duty.

'Hold on,' he said, 'hold on. Now, Kevin, have you had your tea?'

'Not yet,' I said. 'I expect my uncle will give me something.'

'I'll cut you a sandwich,' said Mr Harrison. He took me through to the back, and there he cut two huge slices of bread, about an inch thick, and a slice of beef that seemed hardly any narrower. The result was the biggest sandwich I'd ever seen.

'Get y'self round that,' ordered Mr Harrison. It was quite a task, because the sandwich was almost too big for my mouth. Mr Harrison gave me a glass of milk as well. By the time I had finished, Mike had brought his gleaming motor-bike round to the street in front of the shop, and was gazing at it fondly.

'Lovely bike,' he said as I mounted the pillion behind him. 'Goes like a bomb.'

9 BEFORE I could get my breath we were roaring
through the streets. For the next quarter-hour I
forgot all my worries; I was fully occupied with
holding on for dear life. I was vaguely aware of
shooting along the main road, rattling on the
stone setts and occasionally bouncing in the
tram-tracks. Then there were a few minutes
travelling at a more sedate pace while a police
car was in view, and I could see that we were
heading out towards the country. The police car
turned off, and Mike put on speed again. A few
more breakneck minutes, and we came into a
quiet, suburban-looking area, where the roads
were lined with neat little houses, each in its own
garden. This, I learned later (for it was impossible to ask Mike any questions at the time), was
the Scarsholme Estate. We drew up at a big
Tudor-style pub, set well back from the road, and
I could see from the swinging sign that this was
93 the City Arms.

Deafened and dizzy, I got off the bike, and Mike stood it lovingly in a corner of the car-park.

'Where do they play bowls?' he asked a by-stander. We were directed round to the back, and there indeed were a couple of beautifully kept bowling-greens, on which several games were in progress.

'Old men's marbles!' said Mike scornfully. 'There's not much of a kick in *that*! Give me the bike, any day. . . .'

But I was already inquiring about my uncle. Since the encounter with Mr Harrison, I had become much more hopeful again. I fully expected that everybody would know him and that within a few minutes I should be sitting in his kitchen. I was quite surprised when there were blank looks and a general shaking of heads.

'Never 'eard tell of *'im*!' said an authoritative-looking elder with a silver watch-chain across his waistcoat, who seemed to be looked on as the natural spokesman. 'But of course lots of people come 'ere, and 'appen play in a league game or two, that we don't know the name of. What's 'e like to look at?'

'Quite a big chap,' I said. 'Going a bit grey. Thick eyebrows. Wears glasses.'

'Nay,' said the man with the watch-chain, 'I can't say as I remember a feller like that. Anybody 'ere think they might know 'im?'

But there was another shaking of heads.

'You could try t'Corporation greens,' the man with the watch-chain suggested. 'Plenty of keen bowlers go there. About a mile further up, and bear right at t'new school.'

Mike was quite willing to put his bike through 94

its paces again, and I was getting more used to it. We sped away, and soon arrived at the Corporation bowling-greens. There were half a dozen of them, at the edge of a great park designed to serve the whole Scarsholme area. We talked to several players, and to the man in the Corporation kiosk, but still without result. Eventually someone suggested that we should try the Golden Eagle, which had the only other bowling-greens on the estate.

By now I was growing depressed again, though Mike remained cheerful.

'We'll find him,' he said. 'Just you see, we'll find him. I know these bowls players. My old man's one of them. They never give up playing, they'd rather do without their dinner than without a game. If there's only three lots of greens in Scarsholme, and he doesn't play on two of them, he must play on the other. Come on, Kevin. Mount the faithful steed. Giddy-up, old feller!' (this to the bike.) He kicked the starter, and off we went again.

The Golden Eagle was an old-fashioned inn which they told me later had served Scarsholme when it was 'nobbut a village'. I liked its cheerful, comfortable air. The landlord himself took us round to see his regular bowls players, and once again I gave Uncle Bob's name and description. But any hope that it would be a case of third time lucky faded as once again I looked round the blank faces and watched the shaking of heads.

'You don't want to go by the glasses, you know,' said Mike to the gathering at large. 'He might have stopped wearing them. But has there
95

been anybody here that's big, going grey, and real good at the game – absolutely first class?'

'Don't think so.'

'No.'

'Not that I remember,' came various voices.

As we were about to leave, a small, elderly man came forward.

'You know,' he said thoughtfully, 'there was one feller that came here two or three times, nearly a year ago. Hot stuff, he was. Said he'd be playing regular. But he stopped coming and I haven't seen him since.'

'Aye,' said another. 'I remember t'chap you mean. Sounds a bit like him. He fitted t'description all right.' He pondered for a moment. 'Very quiet-spoken, this feller was that I'm thinkin' of. Very quiet-spoken indeed. But you had a feeling that he could be right tough if it came to a set-to. He used to come here with a crippled lady, pushing her in a wheel-chair.'

'That'll be him!' I cried. For Aunt Flora was a cripple, though she hadn't been in a wheel-chair when I last saw her.

'Do you know where he lives?' asked Mike.

But their faces were blank again. No, they had no idea. They'd only seen him once or twice, they'd never been friends with him exactly. And none of the others could help at all. My momentary elation faded once more as it became clear that we were still up against a blank wall. After a few minutes, Mike turned to me with sympathy in his face.

'Looks like we've had it, Kevin,' he said. 'All we know is that a man who might have been your uncle came here a few times nearly a year 96 ago but nobody knows where he lives or anything about him. Doesn't really get us far, does it?'

'Where do we go from here, then?' I asked miserably.

'Back to my dad's,' said Mike. 'He'll give you some supper anyway, and either a bed or your railway ticket. Cheer up, Kevin, it's not all that bad.'

But it seemed bad enough to me as once again I climbed on to the pillion. This time I was too depressed even to be frightened, and certainly too depressed to know or care where we were going. I was surprised when after a few minutes Mike pulled up.

'Lost my way,' he said briefly. 'Every road looks alike round here. See anyone we can ask?'

I didn't at first. We waited a moment or two. And then a figure appeared, a figure of a man with a letter in his hand, heading no doubt for the pillar-box at the next corner.

The man came towards us and I was about to go up to him when I suddenly stopped. The figure was familiar. A big man. A man wearing spectacles. A man whose hair was beginning to go grey. Surely it couldn't be . . . ?

'Uncle Bob!' I shouted at the top of my voice.

The man stopped, startled. Then:

'Eh, it's Kevin!' he exclaimed.

We stared at each other. There was a moment's silence.

'Is there owt wrong, lad?' my uncle asked, with a note of alarm. For suddenly I was feeling ill. I felt the colour drain from my face. My surroundings blurred. My uncle put an arm round me and seated me on a garden wall. As if from a great distance I heard Mike's voice say:

'He'll be all right in a minute.'

And so I was.

A few minutes later I was sitting in Uncle Bob's parlour before a roaring fire. Mike was beside me, and crippled Aunt Flora was there too. They semed to be waiting until I was fully recovered before questioning me. So I got in first.

'When's the next train to Cobchester?' I asked.

'Next train to Cobchester!' my unce exclaimed. 'When, tonight?'

'Yes, tonight,' I said. 'I've got to go back there. And you, too.'

My uncle leaned forward.

'Come on, Kevin lad,' he said. 'There's summat serious t'matter, isn't there? Out with it, right away!'

'Well . . .' I said. I hesitated for a moment. And then I told the whole story – or nearly the whole story, for some instinct told me to say nothing yet about the gang and the packing-cases. But I described how we had been left alone, how we had discovered Gumble's Yard and organized our moonlight flit, how we had fended for ourselves and attempted to make some money to live on, and finally our meeting with Tony Boyd and the brief time-limit he'd given us. I didn't embroider the tale, but even so it took a good five minutes to tell, and during that time nobody spoke except me.

I went on to describe my search for Uncle Bob himself, and when I mentioned the conversation at the Golden Eagle my uncle made his only interruption.

'Aye,' he said, 'I was hoping to have a game here now and again, but your auntie's not been too well.'

There was a brief silence. Then:

'It's at five past nine,' said my uncle.

'What is?'

'Next train. Now, Flora lass, I'll have to leave you for a day, or 'appen two. You'll be all right, won't you? I'll ask Mrs Morris next door to look in whenever she can. I'm off to Cobchester with Kevin.'

10

'CAMELLIA 2491,' said a voice. It sounded like Dick's. I pressed button A.

'Is that the Reverend Anthony Boyd's house?' I asked.

'Kevin!' said Dick's voice eagerly. 'Kevin! Did you find your uncle? You did? And he's coming. Wizard! Listen, Kevin, Tony's out just now, but they're all right. Sandra and the others, I mean. They're all right! You're all going to be all right!'

The shrilling of a train letting off steam drowned his next few words. I was ringing from Ledford station. Uncle Bob waited on the platform outside the box. In another five minutes we would be on our way.

'What time will you get here?' Dick was asking when I could hear him again.

'Ten-twenty at Cobchester Central.'

'Fine. You'll catch the half-past-ten bus, with a bit of luck. I'll tell Tony and we'll meet you at the bus-stop. Kevin, you're a dimwit. He left a note for you, and I expect you were in such a panic you didn't look at it. Anyway, you've done the right thing. I'll tell you everything when you get here. And Kevin, have you told your uncle about that gang?'

'Not yet,' I said.

'Oh, good. Well, don't. Listen, Kevin, I want to have a private word with you when you arrive. I've found out an awful lot. We're going to have some excitement!'

Excitement, I thought as I put back the receiver, was something I could manage without. What I really wanted was a good long rest.

I slept all the way to Cobchester.

11 THE bus drew up at the north end of Hibiscus Street. I got down, and Uncle Bob followed me. It was a quarter to eleven, and the night was fine and clear with almost a full moon. My uncle and I hadn't talked much – partly because I'd slept all through the train journey and partly because he isn't much of a talker at any time. But it was an enormous comfort to me to have him there. He is a slow man: slow-moving and slow-thinking, and I don't believe he has the least bit of imagination. And yet he is so big and solid, so absolutely honest, so reliable, that you can't help having confidence in him.

Tony and Dick weren't at the bus-stop, but we'd only gone a few yards down Hibiscus Street when we met them. I introduced my uncle, and he and Tony shook hands.

'I'm very relieved to see you,' said Tony. 'Between us I hope we shall be able to sort out these young people's problems. They certainly deserve a happy ending.'

'We'll find a home for all of them together, come what may,' said my uncle stoutly.

They looked at each other with interest. I could tell right away that Tony was favourably impressed by my uncle. I wasn't quite so sure what my uncle thought of Tony. When I'd told him of the Reverend Anthony Boyd, I don't think he'd expected to meet so young and brisk a man.

'I'm sure you'd like to see the place where they've been living,' Tony said to my uncle. 'All the same, I wonder if you could spare the time for a quiet talk with me before we go down there. Let's just go round to the little café in Camellia Hill, and I'll tell you over a cup of coffee what I've been thinking.'

'You won't be wanting us, will you?' Dick asked him.

I was surprised. It's not like Dick to keep out of any conference unless he's thrown out. If there's one thing he loves, it's being right in the middle of things.

'I think we might manage without you,' said Tony, with just a trace of irony.

'Well, Kevin and I will go straight down to the Homestead, then,' said Dick. 'You know the way, Tony. You can follow on when you've had your talk. Oh, and by the way, can I tell Kevin about you-know-what?'

'I'd rather you didn't,' said Tony, and turning to me he went on: 'I've something important to tell you, Kevin, but I'd like to wait until we've a little time together to discuss it. Later tonight, perhaps.'

'Is it about Sandra and the others?' I asked him.

'It's about all of you,' said Tony.

'They're not down at Gumble's Yard now?'

'No, they're spending the night at Sheila's. I'll tell you all about it later on.'

'Come along, Kevin,' urged Dick, tugging at my sleeve. And we continued alone towards Gumble's Yard, while Tony and Uncle Bob turned back the other way towards Aunt Annie's café in Camellia Hill. As soon as they were out of earshot, Dick began to speak rapidly in a low voice.

'I know exactly what that gang are up to,' he told me.

'How?' I asked, baffled.

'It was a bit of luck, really,' said Dick. 'After you left to catch the train I stayed in the Homestead for a while, looking at those electric irons. There were twenty-four of them, all in boxes, packed inside the big case. Well, I had a feeling that one of them might be different from the others, just the same as the packing-case we took was different from all the rest. And I was quite right, too. One of the boxes had a red-pencil cross on it.'

'What was in it?' I asked.

'Oh, an electric iron, just like all the others.'

I was disappointed. 'Is that all?' I asked.

'No,' said Dick triumphantly, 'that's not all. There was a passport as well.'

'A passport?' I was more baffled than ever.

'A passport of the Republic of Santa Lucia, in the name of Pedro Gomez.'

'And what does that mean?'

'Well, what do you know about the Republic of Santa Lucia?'

'Nothing,' I said frankly. Geography to me was just an hour that I had to endure under Mr Jones.

'Well, I'll tell you something about it,' said Dick. 'It's a little country in Central America. It makes a living by registering ships at cut prices, and selling fancy postage stamps, and things like that. Also, it gives its citizenship to anybody, at a price. A lot of the world's leading crooks have a Santa Lucian passport.'

'And who is this Pedro Gomez?'

'You can bet it's a fictitious name,' said Dick. 'It's about as common as John Smith. The point is this, Kevin, and I must say you're jolly slow on the uptake: the passport has been sent here to get someone out of the country.'

'I'm not so slow as all that,' I said. 'If you're sending somebody a passport in a false name, do you have to send about a thousand electric irons along with it?'

'Well, that's a point,' said Dick condescendingly. 'But the fact is, the passport throws light on the irons. You know what those irons are?'

'No, I don't.'

'Unofficial exports.'

'Oh, stop talking in riddles, Dick,' I said impatiently. 'What do you mean by that?'

'Now look,' said Dick. 'Here's a passport, obviously designed for somebody who's getting out of the country. Why should anybody leave the country by way of Gumble's Yard?'

'Go on, you tell me,' I said.

'Because,' said Dick, 'it's on the canal, the 106

North-west Junction Canal. The canal is disused, but it isn't derelict. You can still get along it. Now if you go westward for about a mile, you come to Winsway. And you know what Winsway's on?'

'The Sea Canal.'

'Right,' said Dick. He was enjoying himself. 'Now suppose you have a ship that's outward bound, a ship that's cleared the customs, a ship that's travelling slowly down the Sea Canal at night. And suppose you have a barge with a little cargo that you're thinking of sending abroad. . . .'

'Oh!' I cried, as light came flooding in at last.

'You see now?' said Dick. 'Unofficial exports. Stolen goods, no doubt. It's a way of getting them out of the country. That'll explain the electric irons, I think. But there are other kinds of unofficial export, and the passport's connected with that. I mean the unofficial export of people – the sort of people who carry Santa Lucian passports and call themselves Gomez.'

'And who would they be?'

'Well, people wanted by the police, for instance. Or people who've committed some crime, and need to get away quickly.'

A thought crossed my mind.

'Or gaolbreakers?' I asked.

'Could be,' said Dick.

My mind was turning to the story I'd seen in the newspaper that I'd picked up on the train. I tried to recall the details. The baby-faced criminal Flick Williams, convicted after the burglary at Westley Hall when the Westley diamonds vanished, had escaped from Cobchester Gaol. He had served only a month of his sentence. The diamonds had never been recovered.

Flick Williams. Flick . . .

Suddenly another piece of the jigsaw fell into place.

That page of a letter addressed to someone called Flick, that Dick had found in the Homestead before we came. And the newspaper cutting about Lady Westley that had been with it.

'That's it!' I exclaimed with conviction. 'Flick Williams! This must be his escape route. And he'll probably have the diamonds as well!'

Now it was Dick's turn to be baffled.

'The gaolbreaker!' I said. 'The man who got away from Cobchester Gaol today. He's the person who was in the Homestead before us!'

Dick, who hadn't seen the newspaper story, didn't quite grasp the point, but I had to postpone explaining it for a minute or two because we were now approaching Gumble's Yard. We looked all round us with great caution. There was no sign of men or vehicles. Nevertheless my heart thumped wildly as we went up through the trapdoor.

The table was piled with electric-iron boxes, and lying among them was the passport.

'Did you just leave it lying around like that?' I asked, horrified.

'Why not? Nobody was likely to come.'

'That's what *you* think,' I said. 'Listen, Dick, there's no doubt about it. The man that passport is intended for is Flick Williams, who knew about the Homestead before we came, and who's broken out of Cobchester Gaol today. I saw it in the evening paper. He can't have been down here yet, or the passport wouldn't still be on this table. He's probably lying low all day. But he might arrive any minute now!'

'Then we'll catch him!' cried Dick excitedly.

I flared up.

'Don't be so daft!' I snapped. 'Maybe you think of being a hero, but I reckon we're in a sticky position.'

Even as I spoke, the light had been dying out of Dick's face. No doubt it had occurred to him that a dangerous, and possibly armed, criminal might be more than a match for the two of us.

'I wish Tony and Uncle Bob would come,' I said.

'We'd better go back to meet them,' said Dick, 'if the coast's still clear.'

I went over to the window and peered out through the grime.

'Oh, help!' I cried in dismay.

'What's up?' asked Dick. 'Is the man coming?'

'No,' I said. 'He's not coming. Harold is.'

A small figure was crossing the patch of waste land outside. In the clear moonlight there was no doubt that it was Harold. But it was the new Harold we'd seen in the last two or three days, and instead of his usual jaunty step he walked at a dragging dejected pace.

'He must have sneaked out of Sheila's, just as he did out of here the other night,' said Dick.

I watched with concern until Harold was too close to be seen from above. Then I opened the trapdoor and prepared to help him up. In a moment he was standing between us. His face was white and strained, and he had been crying a good deal. Forgetting our danger for a moment, I recalled my anxiety over Harold. He had suffered more than any of us.

'What is it, Harold?' I asked him gently.

But I couldn't get any sense out of him. 'It's not her I want!' he said two or three times in a strangled voice, and then: 'I haven't got anywhere to *be*.' He was trembling. I put my arm round him.

'You still want your dad, don't you?' I asked.

Harold nodded. His eyes were full of tears. For a moment I wondered whether to tell him we'd seen Walter. I didn't know whether that would do good or harm. Then Dick broke in:

'Look here,' he said. 'We'd better all get away while we can. Let's fetch Tony and your Uncle – and the police.'

I squeezed Harold's hand.

'Come on, lad,' I told him. 'We've got to get out of here quickly. I'll tell you what it's about later.'

Down we went once more through the cottage below. At the doorway we halted while Dick looked cautiously round. This had come to feel like nothing more than a routine, because we had never yet seen anybody about at the times when we wanted to get out. But tonight Dick drew back rapidly.

'Upstairs again!' he hissed. 'There's somebody coming!'

'It'll be Uncle Bob and Tony,' I suggested.

'No. A man and a woman, I think.'

We hurried back to the Homestead and closed the trap. Dick and I went straight to the window. Harold, quite bewildered, sat on the bed.

Two figures, a man's and a woman's, were just turning from Canal Street on to the waste ground. We watched them with interest. I didn't think we knew either of them. But as they advanced it struck me that there was something a little strange about this unknown woman's walk – nothing you could put your finger on, but it just didn't seem quite usual.

I was straining my eyes to see better when a light van, unlit, came tearing down Canal Street at a great pace. It turned across the waste ground and slowed down as it overtook the two walkers. A door swung open and with a leap of remarkable agility the feminine figure was aboard.

On came the van, round the cottages, and we heard it draw up at the back, between the cottages and the canal. I felt the blood drain from my face. Dick and I moved over to the back window. Three figures, including the woman's, emerged from the van and stood directly beneath us. The other two were the man with the tiny moustache and the big man from the barge. Walter was not there.

A minute later the second of the two walkers joined them. All four now began to argue, quietly but furiously. With great caution Dick opened the window slightly, so that we could hear them better. And my heart missed a beat when a voice came from the feminine figure. It was light, smooth, menacing – and unmistakably masculine.

The words from the newspaper story came back to me again: 'Baby-faced criminal Flick Williams.' Dick and I looked at each other in wordless agreement. There could be no doubt that this was the gaolbreaker, and that to help him escape he had adopted female disguise.

'What I mean to find out,' said the smooth, dangerous voice, 'is what happened to the marked case.'

'I've told you,' said the big man in a surly tone, 'I never knew of any marked case and I never saw one.'

'Nor did I,' said the man who had unloaded the cases with Walter. 'In the dark as usual.' He spat disgustedly on the ground. 'Come on, Flick, tell us what it's all about.'

'Now listen,' said Flick. 'Snelson arranged this load in Birmingham, as you know. He had one or two items of, shall we say, personal pro- perty of mine that had to be sent up here. But he couldn't use the post, and he wasn't sure that all of you could be trusted.'

'You lookin' at me, Flick?' asked the man who had spoken last.

'I'm not looking at anybody,' said Flick. 'I'm just telling you that Snelson had his doubts. So he put this – er – property inside one of the cases, and made a red-pencil mark on the out-side so it could be identified. And he telephoned Harris at Winsway to tell him to look out for it. But Harris says that when the barge arrived at Winsway there was no marked case. That's so, isn't it, Harris?' And Flick turned to the fourth man, who had not so far spoken.

'That's right,' said Harris.

'Well, I trust Snelson,' said Flick. 'Oh yes, I trust Snelson. I trust him for many reasons, one of them being that I've only got to open my mouth to have him sent down for fifteen years.' 112

His gaze wandered round the group and back to Harris.

'And I trust you, don't I, Harris?' he went on, with a faint undertone of menace.

'You can trust me,' said Harris shortly.

'So,' said Flick slowly, 'Snelson dispatched a marked case, and Harris didn't get it. And only three men handled the load in between. There was you, Vince' (he looked at the man who'd driven the lorry), 'and you, Rod' (looking at the big fellow). 'And there was the new man . . . what's his name? . . . Thompson. Where is he now?'

'He'll be here with the barge at eleven-thirty,' said Harris.

'He doesn't know anything,' said Vince. 'And the cases we got were all passed on to Rod. We didn't keep any of them back.'

'Somebody,' said Flick coldly, 'is holding out on me. And it looks as though the man with the best opportunity to do the dirty was you, Rod.'

'I'm tellin' you I never saw no marked case,' repeated the big man, his voice rising.

Flick began to say something, but Rod interrupted. Anger seemed to be boiling up inside him.

'If I was you, Flick,' he said thickly, 'I wouldn't call Rod Ridgway a liar.' He rolled up a sleeve, baring a brawny forearm.

'Don't threaten me, Rod,' said Flick smoothly. 'I don't like it much. Do you know how I came to be called Flick?'

In the moonlight there was no mistaking the gleam of steel in his hand.

'Come off it, both of you,' said Harris roughly. This'll get you nowhere, Flick – except back inside.'

'Very well,' said Flick. 'Now, how many cases were loaded on to the lorry in the first place?'

'Snelson told me four dozen,' said Harris.

'And how many were loaded into the barge?'

'Didn't count them,' said Vince.

'You didn't count them,' said Flick contemptuously.

While these exchanges were going on, the big fellow had been simmering, a scowl all over his face. Now he interrupted

'Them cases were lying in the cottage here all night.'

'Oh, they were?' said Flick. 'Contrary to instructions, of course.'

'Somebody else might have taken one,' Rod continued.

'It doesn't sound likely to me,' said Flick. 'Why should anybody take a packing-case from Gumble's Yard – just one? And why the important one? Have you seen anybody around?'

'No,' said Vince. He paused a moment. 'Except that when I came down here a few days ago there seemed to be a lot of kids hanging about. Had a den somewhere around, I dare say.'

'A den,' said Flick softly. 'A den. Now I wonder...'

He looked upward at the cottages, then made a quick movement forward. Suddenly he was shinning up the drainpipe, as Dick had done when we first came to Gumble's Yard. A quick side-step, a toehold where the brick was missing, and he was on the window-sill. In a moment we saw the smooth bony face, evil under a blonde female wig, peering in at us through the grimy window. Then up went the sash, and Flick put a foot through into the room.

I drew away instinctively. But not Dick. Dick went boldly forward, and as Flick brought his head and shoulders under the raised window Dick shoved him back with every ounce of strength.

Falling from the window-sill, Flick grabbed at Dick, but could only get hold of his jacket. A bit of it parted with a rip, having held long enough to break Flick's fall. He landed feet first on the ground below, fell forward, but was not hurt and picked himself up at once.

'Get out!' hissed Dick to me. 'Down through the trapdoor, as quick as you can. They don't know about it. Harold, hide in the cottage and don't move. Kevin, you dash for help. I'll keep them busy as long as possible.'

12

I WENT down through the trapdoor first, and turned to catch Harold as he jumped. His fingertips were hardly clear of the opening before Dick had closed the trap. I knew he would drag the rug across, in the hope that the trapdoor wouldn't be seen if an invasion from outside succeeded.

'You crouch in that corner!' I said to Harold. 'They won't find you there.' I tried to sound confident. And then I hurried to the doorway.

Before me was the stretch of open ground that lay between Gumble's Yard and Canal Street. Crossing it was my biggest hazard. I glanced each way as I went out. For the moment all was clear; the men were still at the canal side of the cottages. But the risk was enormous. I was glad of my plimsolls, which were unlikely to be heard. And I sprinted as fast as I could go across the open space, imagining every second that someone would come round the side of the cottages and see me.

As I reached Canal Street, breathless after the fastest hundred yards I'd ever run, I thought I heard a shout, but I didn't turn my head.

A second or two later I heard the engine of the van being started.

'They must be after me!' I thought, and instead of heading for Hibiscus Street I cut into a deserted warehouse yard. There I crouched behind the wall, breathing hard. I could still hear the van's engine, and it sounded to me as if the vehicle had moved, braked, and moved again, but was still at the other side of the open space. Then the engine stopped and there was silence.

I waited a few moments and peeped out. The van had not been chasing me. It was now parked in front of the row of cottages instead of behind, and, as I watched, two men scrambled on to its roof. I realized what they were doing. They were making a flank attack on Dick by way of the other window. And Dick wouldn't be able to hold out for long on two fronts.

Though the two men looked fully occupied, I decided not to risk re-emerging into Canal Street. I crossed the warehouse yard, climbed the wall at the other side, and sped along an alleyway into Hibiscus Street. As I entered it, St. Jude's clock struck the quarter. A quarter past eleven. It was still not quite half an hour since I'd left Uncle Bob and Tony, though so much had happened that it seemed an age. I thought I might now meet them any minute, but I didn't. I ran the length of Hibiscus Street, then up

Camellia Hill, and finally into Aunt Annie's Café.

As I panted in through the doorway, they were sitting opposite each other at a corner table, each with two empty coffee-cups beside him. It seemed astonishing that on a night of such excitement they should be sitting there quite calm and unconcerned. But of course they had no idea what was going on.

'Well, if you can take responsibility for them ...' I heard Tony say; and then they saw me and both stared. But even now they didn't get up.

'Now young man, what's all the hurry?' demanded Uncle Bob.

'Come at once!' I gasped. 'Dick's besieged in the Homestead by a gang of crooks. And Harold's hiding. We've got to rescue them!'

'Wait a minute, wait a minute,' said Uncle Bob, puffing at his pipe deliberately. 'What gang is this? Some rival lot of lads, I suppose?'

'No!' I cried. 'Criminals! A gaolbreaker! Flick Williams!'

'Come now, lad, calm down ...' began Uncle Bob. But Tony had started to his feet.

'Look here, Kevin,' he said rapidly, 'you're not joking, are you? Because if so, it isn't funny.'

'I'm deadly serious,' I replied. And in a matter of seconds I'd given them an outline of what had happened.

'Come on, Thompson,' Tony called to my uncle. 'We'll hurry down there right away. Kevin, why didn't you tell us before? ... oh well, never mind. Stay behind and ring the police. And don't follow us. Wait for the police to pick you up. Tell them to come at once, it's urgent.'

He raced into the street, with Uncle Bob running, more heavily, behind him. And they'd hardly disappeared when Aunt Annie herself appeared at the inner door. Aunt Annie is in fact Mrs Clough. She's tall, thin, stooping, going grey, and she wears round, gold-framed spectacles. And she's not the brightest of people.

'Can I use your phone, please?' I cried.

She didn't seem to hear.

'Well, I never!' she said. 'Well, I never did! They haven't paid!'

'They're chasing some crooks,' I said impatiently, 'and I've got to ring the police. So I'd like to use your phone.'

Aunt Annie's mouth dropped open.

'Chasing *what*?' she said.

'Crooks. Criminals. A man who broke out of gaol.'

Aunt Annie gazed, goggle-eyed. I thought she was going to say something. Then she obviously gave the subject up as being beyond her, and returned to the only point she felt sure about.

'They haven't paid,' she repeated.

'Look,' I said. 'That was the Reverend Anthony Boyd, of St. Jude's Church. He wouldn't cheat you, would he? Now *please* let me use your phone.'

But she was still floundering.

'Eh, t'things they get up to, these days. . . .' she began, and then, seeing me on the point of repeating my plea yet again, she seized thankfully upon an excuse and said: 'No, you can't use t'phone. It's too late. I'm closing.'

She wasn't just being awkward, I realized. The 120

situation was too much for her. She didn't know how to cope.

I didn't appeal again. I'd just remembered that there was a call-box halfway down Camellia Hill on the other side. I dashed off, leaving Aunt Annie still gawping.

At the call-box I met with another frustration. Inside it were a couple: a girl who was giggling into the mouthpiece and a young man making passes at her as she did so. That could go on for a long time. Meanwhile the minutes were passing.

I felt a brief panic. Then I remembered that there was another call-box, well down Hibiscus Street, at the corner of Mimosa Row. I raced away once more. And this time I saw, thankfully, that the box was empty.

I got through almost at once, and the response was immediate. A brisk voice asked the essential questions and said that a couple of cars would be on the way in no time. 'You stay where you are,' the voice concluded, 'and they'll pick you up.'

'They needn't bother,' I said. 'They can go straight down to Gumble's Yard. I'll be there.' And I rang off, quickly.

13

At the corner of Canal Street I stopped and peered cautiously ahead. It was still bright moonlight, and the cottages of Gumble's Yard were clearly outlined. There was no sign of activity, and not a sound to be heard. I don't know quite what I'd expected to find, but there was something sinister about the silence.

I ran along Canal Street until I was facing the cottages across the patch of open ground. Then I stopped again, my heart thumping and my legs suddenly weak. I realized that I was afraid to go on. I felt furious over my own cowardice. I reminded myself of the valiant heroes of innumerable books that I'd read. I told myself fiercely that Dick wouldn't have hesitated for a moment. But my legs just wouldn't move. It struck me that I could easily wait for the police cars after all. And I think I would have done so if I hadn't heard a voice crying shrilly:

'No! No! Don't!'

It was Sandra's.

I didn't stop to wonder what Sandra was doing down there. I found that I had the use of my legs after all. I ran at top speed across the waste ground and in through the doorway of the cottage where I'd left Harold.

Inside, all was dark and quiet. Harold was not there. The trapdoor was still closed. No sound came from above. I was about to go up when I heard from outside – the side nearer the river – a shout of 'Get back!' It sounded like Flick. I darted to the door again and edged my way round the outside of the row of cottages until I came to the corner nearest the canal. And then I jumped back silently in fright, for I found myself just behind Flick and his companions.

Fortunately they were all looking the other way, engrossed in whatever they were watching. I returned to the cottage, and this time I climbed up to the trap-door and, slowly and cautiously, began to push it up. There was no reaction from above, so I pushed the trap aside and put my head through. The Homestead was empty. But what a mess! Everything had been turned upside down, the beds were stripped, the table lay on its side, and all our possessions were strewn over the floor. Both windows were broken, and pieces of glass lay everywhere. The Santa Lucian passport was gone.

I crept to the window-frame at the canal side and looked out. And now I saw what was happening. Immediately below me, in a little knot, were Flick and two of his three men; Vince was not there. Close beside them, Dick lay slumped 124 on the ground, face down. He might have been dead for all I could see, or for all the notice they took of him. With horror I saw that Flick was holding Sandra in front of him, shield-like. And once again there was a sinister gleam of metal in his hand.

'Back ... back. ...' I heard him call. And further along the bank, my Uncle Bob and Tony moved slowly backwards

'That'll do,' said Flick, when they were twenty or thirty yards away. 'Don't move now. If you come nearer, or if you run for it, you know what'll happen And if you don't think I'd really use this knife, just you try.' The last three words were loaded with menace.

I drew back from the window. I had forgotten my own panic now, but I was sick with fear on Sandra's behalf. Flick, I knew, was a desperate man with little to lose. I had seen him threatening one of his own associates less than an hour ago. If Tony and Uncle Bob attacked, I had no doubt that Sandra would suffer. And even if they held back, the arrival of the police cars could not be long delayed and was likely to have the same result.

Nevertheless, I thought, things looked black for Flick. Whatever injuries he might inflict on anyone, he hadn't a hope of getting away. Or had he? In the momentary silence a new sound came to my ears and reminded me that the game was by no means up. It was the put-put of the approaching barge, making its way unlit along the black surface of the canal.

'Stay where you are!' cried Flick to my uncle and Tony as the barge drew nearer. 'This little girl can come for a ride with us. If there's any pursuit, it will hurt her more than it hurts me.' Again the note of menace sent shivers down my spine. 'You'll see her again tomorrow, if you're all good,' Flick concluded.

The church clock struck the half-hour, and as it did so the barge – exactly on time – bumped gently against the quay. Flick and his companions turned their heads in its direction. For an instant their wariness was relaxed. I saw Dick, who was still lying flat on the ground, raise his head and glance rapidly round. And I realized that, though apparently helpless, he was at least fully conscious.

Suddenly it came home to me that I was the only person who could tackle Flick. No one else could do anything except at the risk of Sandra's life. But I was unseen. All I needed was a suitable weapon: something to throw. I am a pretty smart out-fielder, and given a cricket-ball I could have hit Flick easily at twice the range.

I looked around me. Of course there was no such thing handy. But my fingers closed upon the base of an electric iron, the one that Dick had unpacked. An electric iron is not the best of missiles, because it's an awkward shape, and difficult to throw straight. There was a risk that Flick would move at the vital moment, or that I should simply miss him. There was even a risk of hitting Sandra instead. On the other hand, the range was short. And it was my only chance. I raised my arm and, with a rapid prayer, I threw as hard and straight as I knew how.

It was a perfect shot. I think it would have felled Flick, but some premonition caused him 126

to move his head at the last split-second. The iron hit him a glancing blow and fell to the ground. Flick staggered sideways. And at that moment Dick sprang to his feet and with a superhuman effort grabbed the wrist that held the knife.

Then everything happened at once. Flick's associates launched themselves on Dick. Uncle Bob and Tony rushed into the fray. Sandra had torn herself loose. I leaned out of the window.

'Run, Sandra, run!' I shouted at the top of my voice.

Then down I went through the trapdoor. Sandra hadn't run far. I met her in the cottage doorway.

'Go on,' I urged her. 'Get away from here, quick!'

'Don't be so daft!' snapped Sandra. She didn't look like someone who'd just been in danger of her life. 'I came down here to find Harold, and I'm going to find him.'

I didn't stop to argue. 'All right,' I said. 'You look for him. But keep out of trouble. I'm going to help the others.'

I hurried round to the canal bank. It was like a rugby scrum there, as half a dozen bodies swayed to and fro, perilously near to the water's edge. Dick was still holding Flick's wrist with both hands, and Uncle Bob had grabbed Flick's free arm. Flick's friends were trying to drag the two of them away from him. Tony was, for the moment, on the fringe, and as I dashed up I saw him launch a perfect straight right at the big, bull-like man they called Rod. Wrong tactics, I thought. Rod shook it off unmoved, and went on to heave Uncle Bob away from Flick with a wrestler's throw. At the same moment a man scrambled from the barge on to the wharf. It was Walter. He stood at the edge of the fray, as if undecided whether to join in.

Flick now seemed to be getting the better of things. He was still holding the knife. The big man grabbed Dick and by brute force removed his grasp on Flick's wrist. Uncle Bob was still on the ground. Tony was struggling with the third man, Harris. Flick leaped to his feet and there was a gleam of light as the knife flashed round in his hand.

And now I heard a clear, high-pitched voice ring out above the sounds of the scuffle.

'Dad!' it called. 'Dad! Dad!'

Harold came running from the outhouse, where he must have been hiding, and headed straight for the struggling group. Flick swung round. And in that instant a heavy boot lifted the knife out of his grip and sent it flying through the air. It was Walter. He had intervened – and on our side.

I saw the knife fall, grabbed it, and hurled it into the canal. Then I seized Harold's arm and dragged him out of danger. Sandra had heard his cry, and came running round to take charge of him. Meanwhile the struggle went on. It was now a matter of kicking, punching, and gouging. Flick and his friends still had the advantage. The big man in particular was a powerful fighter. The tactics of the gang were now to disengage themselves and get away.

'On to the barge!' I heard Flick cry; and a
moment later Harris jumped and landed on it

safely. Flick was surrounded, but again the big man came to his rescue. He felled Uncle Bob with a blow, and landed a vicious kick in Dick's stomach. Flick, with a ducking, twisting movement, threw Tony off balance, and neatly tripped Walter. Flick and Rod were now both free. Rod jumped to the barge. Flick turned to follow him. But he was not quick enough. Walter was on his feet instantly and charged, head down.

On the very edge of the wharf Flick lost his footing. There was a shout, then a splash. And then came the put-put of the barge. Flick's friends were not waiting for him.

Flick came to the surface. 'Help! Help! I can't swim!' I heard him cry.

'Let 'im drown!' growled Walter.

But Tony was already stripping, and a moment later had dived into the black, unappetizing water. As he did so, there came the sound of vehicles approaching at high speed. The headlights of a car swept across the scene. A second car followed, and both of them crunched to a halt. And when a dripping, half-conscious Flick Williams, in what remained of his woman's clothing, was hauled on to the wharf, it was the strong arm of the police officers that took care of him.

As everyone clustered round, I found myself next to Dick, and noticed that he had retrieved the electric iron I had thrown at Flick.

'What d'you want that for?' I asked.

Dick said nothing, but grinned wanly.

'Anyway, what happened to you?' I went on.

'I was knocked out, that's all,' said Dick. 'First, two of them invaded the Homestead from the 130 other side. I knew I couldn't fight on both fronts, so I jumped out of the window. There were two more down below, though, and they were too much for me. Still, I put up a good fight.'

'You were lucky not to be stabbed,' I said.

'Sandra was luckier,' said Dick. 'She came running down – looking for Harold, I suppose – and dashed in to the rescue.'

'She's a brave girl,' I said, thinking of my own fear a few minutes before.'

'Mad!' said Dick. 'Absolutely mad. I don't know what we'll do with her.' But the tone in his voice was one of admiration.

My sense of shame overwhelmed me, and I felt I had to confess to Dick how I'd hung back at the other side of the waste ground. But when I'd told him, Dick stared at me.

'Why, you were splendid, Kevin,' he said. 'It was you who made all the difference.'

A grin crossed his face.

'If you want to talk about cowardice,' he said, 'the driver, Vince, is the best example. He didn't fancy a scrap. When your Uncle and Tony appeared, he dashed for his van and cleared off, quick.'

Then Dick peered at me and asked, with sudden seriousness:

'Kevin, are you all right?'

'I'm fine,' I said. But as I said it I realized that I wasn't fine at all. A wave of dizziness came over me. I beat it back.

'I'll sit down,' I said, and I half sat, half fell. All that was going on around me suddenly seemed very far away. The wave of blackness returned, and this time I couldn't be bothered to beat it back.

Of the next hour's events I have only a vague recollection, for although I soon came round I was half dead with shock and exhaustion. The day which had begun with my paper round and had included the journey to Ledford and back, as well as the events on the wharf, seemed to have been going on for ever.

Three memories, however, stand out from the confusion.

One was of Harold, clasped in Walter's arms, sobbing with relief and joy. For Walter – scraggy, dirty, unshaven, dishonest Walter – was his dad, and that was all that mattered to him.

The second was of a brisk, official voice asking:

'Where do these children live?' There was a brief hesitation, and then a reply from Walter:

'They live with me. Forty, Orchid Grove.'

The last, and most vivid of all, was Dick calling a police inspector over and showing him the electric iron, from which he had just removed the base.

'Look at this,' Dick said in a casual tone, as if showing somebody a stamp from his collection. Within the iron, neatly coiled where the element should have been, was a row of stones. Precious stones. Diamonds. In fact, as the inspector said with awe in his voice, 'The Westley Diamonds!'

14

IT was broad daylight. I was lying on a sofa with blankets tucked round me. But where was I?

'How about some breakfast, Kevin?' called a cheerful voice. It was Tony's. Yes, of course, I had been brought to his lodgings for the night. And whatever time was it now? I glanced at the clock on the mantelpiece. Eleven!

'My paper round!' I exclaimed.

'Don't worry about that!' said Tony. 'Dick said he'd see to it. He's tough, that lad.'

'Tougher than I am,' I said ruefully. I still felt a little shaky.

'You're to take it easy today,' said Tony. 'The police have a good deal to ask you, but they've agreed to wait until tomorrow. No school, of course. Now, will you have some bacon? And an egg? Two eggs? And why not a bath while I'm cooking them?'

So I had a bath, and then I sat in a dressing-gown of Tony's and ate bacon and two eggs which I'd never had in my life before. It was like being a millionaire. Afterwards I got into my own clothes, feeling much better.

'Where's Uncle Bob?' I asked. I remembered vaguely that he too had come to Tony's to spend the night.

'He's gone round to Sheila's,' Tony said. 'Sandra slept there. Your uncle's going to buy her a present. Something nice, I hope. She's a remarkable girl, your sister.'

I didn't contradict him.

'Look here, Tony,' I said thoughtfully 'What's going to become of us? We can't go on living at Gumble's Yard now, can we?'

'You never could have done,' said Tony gently. 'It was only a temporary refuge.'

'Did the police realize we were actually living there?'

'No. They thought it was just a place where you went to play. It may not occur to them to suspect anything else. And if they do, I think they'll let it pass, so long as you're fixed up now.'

'But are we?' I asked. 'I heard Walter saying last night that we lived with him at Forty, Orchid Grove. It sounded as if he was taking us back. But I don't think he could look after us on his own, even if we wanted him to, and I'm not sure that I do.'

'Walter's not such a bad chap as you think,' said Tony. 'I've had a chat with him. He's weak, of course, and easily led, but he doesn't really mean any harm.'

'Won't he be in trouble himself?'

'I don't think so. He'd only been working with

that gang for a few days, and didn't know what they were up to. Mind you, he must have realized it was something shady. They were paying him twenty pounds a week – which is a good deal above his usual level – with a berth in the barge thrown in. And all for a bit of labourer's work.'

'Unofficial exports,' I said, recalling Dick's phrase.

'Anyway, his last action paid for all,' said Tony. 'When he came in on our side it made all the difference. He's not without decent feelings, you see.'

'It wasn't so decent to walk out on us in the first place.'

'No, it wasn't. But you probably don't know exactly what happened, Kevin. He walked out on you because Doris had walked out on him. He was weak, you see, as I said before. He couldn't face the responsibility for four of you alone, so he just ran away from the whole problem.'

My eyes widened.

'I certainly didn't know that,' I said. 'But why did Doris walk out? Where did she go? And where is she now?'

'She walked out after a row, because she said she was fed up with him and with the whole lot of you,' said Tony. 'Where she went is something we don't know. She said she was going off with another fellow. But either that wasn't true or the chap wouldn't have her. Sheila found her yesterday, after a bit of detective work, wandering the streets in a distressed state. So we had some excitement, as you can guess, and that's why I was out when you got to my place. That's why Gumble's Yard was empty, too, because we had to bring Sandra into the consultation. And now – well, Doris is back at Orchid Grove, with Walter.'

'And they want us back?'

'So they say.'

There was a moment's pause. Then,

'What do you think, Tony?' I asked hesitantly.

Tony looked me straight in the eye.

'I think,' he said, 'that you should go back to them. They haven't actually ill-treated any of you, have they?'

'No. But they haven't actually treated us well, either. And what if all this happened again?'

'Somehow I don't think it will. I think both of them have had quite a jolt in the last day or two. And we have to face facts, Kevin. Your uncle can't take you all; it's doubtful if he can take any of you, because of his wife's illness. The alternative is for you to be taken into care by the local authority. I know already what you feel about that, and I feel exactly the same. And so indeed would the authorities. Even an unsatisfactory family life is better than none.'

I said nothing. What I was feeling was rather complicated. Up to last week I had just accepted Walter and Doris, the way you accept the weather. I'd known that they weren't exactly wonderful, but they were all we'd got, and we were used to them. Now I was seeing them with new eyes. In particular, I couldn't help comparing them with kindly, straightforward people like Tony and Sheila and my Uncle Bob, or for

that matter like Dick's parents. For Harold and
Jean especially, I thought, it was a pretty rough
deal. I even felt a moment's unfair resentment
towards Tony. What did he know, I thought
bitterly, about what it was like to be dragged
up by such a pair?

Some of this must have shown in my face, because Tony went on:

'I know, Kevin, it's not ideal for you. But
plenty of Cobchester children are still worse off.
And you and Sandra have made good already.
The younger ones have you to look after them
and set an example. They'll grow into nice kids
and be none the worse, just you see. And if things
seem really tough, you're not friendless, you
know. Sheila and I will be glad to help you in
any way we can, and your uncle will keep in
touch with all of us.'

Just then Sandra and Uncle Bob came in.
Sandra had had her hair done and got a new
frock. She looked smarter than I'd ever seen her.
Tony gave a comic whistle. Uncle Bob, un-
ruffled by the previous night's events, was in a
facetious vein, and indulged in a lot of heavy-
handed jokes about all the conquests Sandra
was going to make. I think he was trying to make
her blush. But he didn't know Sandra. Sandra
has never had time to get self-conscious. Then
my uncle told me he meant to buy me some new
clothes too, but I found it hard to get interested.

'Have you spoken to Sandra about this?' I
asked Tony.

'I don't think I need to,' Tony said. And then
he asked Sandra, in a matter-of-fact voice:

'Well, what are you all going to do now?'

'Go on as we did before,' said Sandra without hesitation. 'What else can we do? We'll be all right.'

'You see?' said Tony to me.

Well, I knew they were right; there wasn't any practical alternative. And as usual I was cheered up by Sandra's presence and the thought that we'd be seeing things through together.

'All right,' I said. 'Perhaps we'd better be getting . . .' I hesitated over the last word, and then brought it out firmly, 'home.'

And a few minutes later all four of us were on our way round to Orchid Grove.

A strange sight met us when we arrived. Sheila was there, and she was down on her knees scrubbing the floor. It certainly needed it. The whole place was dirty, and as most of the furniture was still at Gumble's Yard it was also even barer than usual. To see slim, pretty Sheila with a scarf round her head working away for dear life seemed odd, but also in a way rather comforting.

Doris was there, too. She was sitting on the one remaining chair, smoking a cigarette. She didn't get up when we came in.

The new, critical feeling came over me again.

Yes, I thought, that's Doris all over. Sit around and let somebody else do the work. . . .

Then Walter came in from the back, where he'd been doing some odd job. He was quite different in manner; he fussed about a good deal, rather anxiously, and put on a great show of being the conscientious householder. Another chair and some boxes were found, Tony sat on the window-ledge, and a kind of general conference began. All sorts of details were discussed :

food, money, the recovery of the possessions that were in the Homestead. Tony told them all of a plan he had to find a job for Walter. Uncle Bob said he was going to cut down his beer and smokes and would pay our rent as a contribution towards keeping the home going. There was a general air of starting afresh. In the middle of it all, Harold and Jean came in. Dick was with them, but he tactfully withdrew on finding the place so crowded. Jean rushed to Sandra and sat on her knee. Harold had eyes only for his father.

Doris was the only one who took no part in the proceedings. She sat looking dully at nothing in particular. On her flabby face there was no expression at all. More bitter thoughts came to me. The truth was, I realized suddenly, that Doris was simply not equal to things. She wasn't very bright or very energetic or very likeable. It was a further development in my understanding. Poor soul, I thought, life's pretty grim for her. We'll have to carry her along somehow.

'Well,' said Walter cheerfully when everything seemed more or less organized, 'we're all going to do fine from now on. No more complaints. And now it's dinner-time. Would anybody like to stay and have dinner here with us? Bob, lend us a dollar, will you? Sandra, just you nip along to the fish shop . . .' And Sandra slipped quietly out, as she'd done a thousand times before, to go to Wade's fish-and-chip shop at the corner.

A few minutes later Sandra and I went out. We'd both breakfasted late that morning and didn't want anything to eat. Tony and Sheila also excused themselves. So we left the rest of them to it, and for a few minutes the four of us walked together: from Orchid Grove to Hibiscus Street, from Hibiscus Street to Camellia Hill, from Camellia Hill to the corner of the Wigan Road.

Tony and Sheila were walking hand in hand, and suddenly I wondered when they were going to get married. So I asked them. Sandra turned on me crossly and said:

'Don't be so rude, you shouldn't ask people that,' but I didn't care. And Tony didn't mind, though he looked grave.

'Not for quite a while,' he said. 'Curates don't get much pay, you know. And Sheila has her elderly parents to look after. So the outlook isn't too promising just now. But the day will come – unless, of course,' and he smiled at Sheila, 'she gets tired of waiting for me and marries somebody else.'

Sheila pulled a face at him.

'So you see,' concluded Tony, 'we can't always have what we want.'

'We can always hope,' said Sandra, in her matter-of-fact tone that often sounds so grown-up.

We left them in the Wigan Road, after Sheila had said she'd come round again next morning to help with the cleaning-up, and I'd made an arrangement with Tony to call on him at the week-end. Then Sandra and I turned back into the Jungle. At the corner of Hibiscus Street we met Dick, and the three of us went on together; not going anywhere in particular but just enjoying each other's company.

It was a fine spring day, not warm but with a sort of hazy sunshine. Summer was coming, and blades of grass were showing between the stone setts, and soon the weeds would blossom on the empty sites. The days were getting longer. Next week perhaps we would be playing cricket after school. There was a dog in Mimosa Row that I was getting very friendly with. I was going to make a soap-box car for Harold. Life was full of interesting things to do.

We walked three abreast, with Sandra in the middle. And as we turned the corner into our own street I felt happy and burst out singing.

'Hark at him!' said Sandra. 'Not a care in the world.'

'Where does it hurt, Kevin?' asked Dick with mock sympathy.

'I'll hurt *you* in a minute!' I said.

And we started a friendly scuffle, the kind that happens a dozen times a day.

ABOUT THE AUTHOR

John Rowe Townsend was born in Leeds, England, and educated at the grammar school there and at Cambridge University, where he took an honours degree in English and edited the undergraduate newspaper. He worked as a journalist on the *Yorkshire Post* and on the London *Evening Standard* before joining the *Manchester Guardian* in 1949. He was editor of the *Guardian*'s weekly international edition for some years.

An active interest in the social conditions of poorer children led to his first book, *Gumble's Yard* (1961). This was followed by *Hell's Edge*, which was a runner-up for the Carnegie Medal in 1963, and *Widdershins Crescent* (which is now published in Puffin under the title *Good-bye to Gumble's Yard*).

Mr Townsend has had a lifelong interest in children's books. Besides reviewing them in the *Guardian* and elsewhere, he has lectured about them in Manchester and Sheffield Universities, and is the author of a study of English children's literature, *Written for Children* (1965).

He has twice spent some time in the United States: as a member of the International Seminar at Harvard and, more recently, as a visiting lecturer at the University of Pennsylvania, at Philadelphia.

Heard about the Puffin Club?

... It's a way of finding out more about Puffin books
and authors, of winning prizes (in competitions),
sharing jokes, a secret code, and perhaps seeing your
name in print! When you join you get a copy of
our magazine, *Puffin Post*, sent to you four times a
year, a badge and a membership book.
For details of subscription and an application form,
send a stamped addressed envelope to:

The Puffin Club Dept A
Penguin Books Limited
Bath Road
Harmondsworth
Middlesex UB7 ODA

and if you live in Australia, please write to:

The Australian Puffin Club
Penguin Books Australia Limited
P.O. Box 257
Ringwood
Victoria 3134